Hidden in Flame

Samantha Lee

Published by Samantha Lee, 2020.

HIDDEN IN FLAME

First edition. August 27, 2020.

ISBN: 9798677770975

Written by Samantha Lee.

Also by Samantha Lee

Mine Series
Release Me
Saved Me

Standalone
Steady Hands
Evanescence
Unapologetic
Hidden in Flame

I began writing this book for my daughter who loves books about dragons. Then my son was dragged into it, so now, this book is for my twins. Finally, mommy wrote a book you can read. You two own my heart, and now I have immortalized it.

CHAPTER ONE

The Beginning

The inside of the cave was black, and the air was humid. Asthmoth heard the shouts from the humans who surrounded the entrance of the cave. Their voices drifted inside and echoed within.

"Come out here and face us, you fowl Beasts of Satan! We aren't afraid of you. Come out and fight us!"

Asthmoth tensed ready to give them the fight they demanded. Then he felt his mate's hands wrap around his waist. "Please don't go, please," Lilah begged her husband.

Asthmoth scoffed her worry away. "These humans are no match for my dragon. They have called me out, and I will answer with fire, tooth, and claw."

"Ah!" Aliah's shrill pierced the depths of the cave and bounced around them. Her pain was intense. Asthmoth turned to face his disgraced daughter, who lay writhing on the cave floor, her stomach large with child. It would have been a joyous occasion, if not for the human at her side. He couldn't stand it.

"Mother, I can't hold her, she comes," his daughter screamed, and his mate unraveled her arms from his waist and ran to her daughter's side.

Asthmoth looked down at his daughter. Even within the darkness of the cave, his dragon sight gave him the ability to penetrate the darkness that surrounded them. He could see the blood that pooled on the unforgiving stone beneath his daughter.

Alarmed at the sight of so much blood, Asthmoth asked his mate, "Is it normal for her to bleed this much?"

His mate clutched their daughter's hand so tight his mate's knuckles were white. It was as though his mate thought by holding their daughter's hand, she could tether their daughter to this world.

His mate shook her head. "I don't know what I should expect with a birth such as this. I," she stuttered. "Have never heard of something like this. If we had more time, then I could have asked the older dragons, if there was anything..."

He saw his mate's eyes widened, and her mouth closed. Then he looked down at his daughter. Her teeth clenched, and a horrid grunt of pain squeezed past his daughter's best defenses.

Asthmoth turned his glare to Duncan, the human his daughter, chose as her mate. The one whose seed was killing his daughter. "This is your fault. You should have never let this happen. Never. Look at her!" Asthmoth yelled, "She is dying."

"Father," his daughter called to him. Her voice nearly inaudible even to his heightened hearing.

"Don't blame him. It's not his fault. I love him and my daughter, even if having her costs me my life. I have no regrets."

His daughter's eyes brimmed with unshed tears, and he nearly relented his anger, but he held fast. How could he not blame the human? Asthmoth frowned down at his daughter. How could she be so stupid to fall for a human? How could she introduce such filth into his bloodline? His pure bloodline.

"I raised you better. I though—"

Duncan interrupted him. "I am sick and tired of having the same argument with you. What's done is done, now, given what is in front of us." He pointed to the entrance where he could still hear the human's demanding they come out and face them. Asthmoth grunted. He'd kill them all with his dragon breath. Duncan continued, "Should we not at least try to bury the hatred between us?"

"How dare you speak to me in this manner, Human?" Asthmoth spat the word human, to ensure Duncan understood what he thought of his kind.

Duncan lifted his chin in defiance. "I dare as Aliah's husband and the father of our child that is coming into this world of discord and prejudice. Now isn't the time to fight each other. We need to think of a plan, so we can all live on."

Asthmoth crossed his muscular arms over his chest and lifted his brow. "And am I to assume you have a plan?"

Duncan yelled, "Asthmoth, don't turn your condescension on me. At least I'm thinking! Which is more than what you are doing and more than I should do, considering my wife is likely dying in front of me!"

As if speaking about Aliah pulled Duncan to her, he turned away from Asthmoth and sat next to her. Asthmoth watched his daughter clench the human's hand and gave him a subtle shake of her head. Even the slight shake of her head seemed to exhaust her.

For the first time, Asthmoth worried. He worried that his daughter would leave him behind. He hoped after she gave birth to the babe, he could have convinced her to leave the child with the man and marry King Thomas' son as she was supposed to so they could preserve the ever-dwindling dragon line. He thought he had time to talk her into it. He couldn't believe she could love a half-breed child once she saw it, but now, he may never get the chance to reconcile with her, and as King, he couldn't bring himself to grovel for her forgiveness in front of her human mate.

Asthmoth ran a hand down his face in frustration.

Another muffled scream came from his daughter, and he turned around so he wouldn't face her. He couldn't stand to watch any further. He would let the women tend to each other and determine the best way to get them out of this situation unscathed. Within a few minutes, he felt a presence next to him. He knew without looking it was Duncan. His human stench traveled to his nostrils before the man appeared.

He heard the human breathe deeply and knew he would disrupt the silence Asthmoth desperately needed.

"Most people don't know that dragons can shapeshift."

"Why would we ever share our secrets with such an inferior species?"

"Right, why would you? Never mind, you won't drag me into an argument, but I think dragon arrogance might work in our favor."

"Our?" Asthmoth asked.

"Yes, our, because my wife and child have a stake in this, which means I do too, and I will fight to the death to protect Aliah and our daughter whether or not you like it, King."

Smoke wafted from Asthmoth's nostrils. He clenched his jaw trying to calm his ire. He would not allow a human to upset him, but Duncan was right. Now was not the time for killing, especially not in front of Aliah, but later, when she wasn't looking, he would breathe fire on him.

Behind him, Asthmoth heard another muffled wail of pain. His body tensed. He stood silent, his back stiff and arms crossed over his chest. Unapproachable and unmovable, the epitome of a dragon. His mind wandered to his knowledge about birthing babes until a shadow covered his mind, gnawing the edges of his fragile hope that his daughter would survive. How long had she been in labor? Five hours or three days, he couldn't say.

Asthmoth sighed. He couldn't figure out a solution aside from fighting their way out, which would only hurt his daughter more. Aliah needed a healer. He had to figure out how to get her to one. The shadow in his mind whispered to him she wouldn't make it; she'd be dead long before they left the cave.

Once again, Duncan breached his space and interrupted his thoughts.

"Asthmoth, I know you hate humans, and I know it pains you that your daughter chose me to be her mate. I know all of this, but I wonder if you could try to understand what your daughter and I accomplished with our union. If we had succeeded in our quest to show the world our love, we would have shown everyone that we could all live in harmony. We wanted the fighting and killing to stop. Dragons are nearly all but wiped out. We were trying to be the example."

Asthmoth snorted. "And look how that turned out for you."

"No, we didn't think the end would come so soon, but I don't regret being with Aliah. She is the love of my life, and she carries the manifestation of our love. How can I be sad about our daughter's birth? I can't, but here we are, surrounded by enemies and facing death if we don't find a solution. My wife or mate, in the language of your people, wants us to choose life. She wants us to leave here and live on. We hoped for the best with Aliah's pregnancy, but we planned for the worst. She made me promise if she didn't survive to-to burn her body in the way of your people."

"No Human can begin the Great Death ritual of dragons. She was foolish to ask you."

"I know that, and so does she, but she didn't think you would be there when she gave birth. Aliah wanted a proud end. She wanted to be one with her people."

Asthmoth shook his head. *Both of them are foolish.*

Asthmoth glanced at Duncan. He'd never seen him so deflated. He hunched his broad shoulders that were once the King's blade, and his movements were sluggish, "I have a plan," he said.

"Let's hear it, Human."

"Why are the villagers upset? What do they want?"

Asthmoth shrugged. How was he to know what humans thought? Their thoughts were of no concern to him.

Duncan waited for a minute before he continued. "King Becklar and his dragons caused chaos to erupt in the skies. They killed many people and destroyed families. The dragons that were once revered became our enemies. The villagers are full of grief, which has mutated into hatred. Now, they seek vengeance from the ones who have hurt them. Vengeance from the ones who they believe are trapped inside this cave."

Annoyed, Asthmoth growled. "Yes, your point, Human."

"What if we gave them the dragon they want? Cooled their blood-lust."

Asthmoth whirled to confront Duncan, snarling, teeth bared in threat. "What do you mean? Do you wish to kill me here? You can try you pathetic human."

Duncan straightened to his full height. Unwavering and unafraid of Asthmoth's anger. "I'm not speaking of you. I am thinking of my wife." Duncan dropped his gaze, but only for a second before he lifted his chin. "The villagers outside are expecting dragons to fly out scales and fire, but what if three humans and a baby run for safety after slaying the enemy dragon?"

Asthmoth shook his head. He wouldn't give up on his daughter so easily. "Aliah will live. She is a dragon, and we do not die easily. Your plan will not work."

"I will not repeat these words, Asthmoth. I can't. The plan is sound, and we both know Aliah will not make it through childbirth. She's lost too much blood. You are a dragon king who has seen many battles. You know better than I what death looks like when it stands in your presence. Do not let my wife's death be for nothing, because if those villagers come in here, my daughter and your daughter will lie among the dead."

Duncan turned and walked back toward Aliah, leaving Asthmoth with his thoughts. How could he sacrifice his daughter to the humans?

DUNCAN WATCHED AS HIS wife lay dying in front of him. A strange mix of grief, pride, and misery overcame him. He bent down and kissed his wife's damp forehead. "My love, I have done as you wished. I have spoken with your father, but it pains me to think of a life without you in it. You must live. Then we will build a home deep in the forest and live there with our daughter and the freedom of the wild. If you fight. If you keep holding on, we can still have this life together."

Duncan looked deep within his wife's unique hazel eyes. He wanted to turn away from her, but he couldn't be a coward in what may be their last minutes together. He held his wife's stare, grateful that by being her mate, she'd made him a little less human. Duncan could see in the dark as well as he could see during the day. He was grateful that he could see the laugh lines around her mouth and her straight, regal nose one last time. He was glad he could look into her hazel eyes and see the love and hope for her people mixed with regret, but not for herself; he knew her better than that; she regretted the pain her passing would cause him.

How could his seed be what took away his wife, who was a beautiful light in a colorless world? He hated himself for agreeing to have a child knowing the risks. He thought, after all the good Aliah had done in the world, the gods owed her a debt. They owed her, and he thought they would pay with a healthy birth, but he was wrong. The gods took more than they gave. Much more.

"Duncan, my love, this is not your fault. I have lived an endless life, and I don't begrudge or fear death. I fear not being here for you and our daughter, but I know you will give her a wonderful life. I'm not a coward, Duncan, you are well aware of that. If I must die, what better reason would there be than saving my people and my daughter? I couldn't ask for a more honorable death. My love, I will gladly run into death's icy embrace if this means the fighting and killing will stop." Softly she said, "We knew this was a possibility. We aren't wrong. You, my love, are not wrong or at fault, please, do not despair."

Duncan sobbed openly. "How can you ask that of me, Aliah? You are my heart. How can you ask me not to despair? My life will not know happiness again. My soul will be forever tormented from the absence of its better half; this is the reality of my life without you. Do not ask me to do the impossible. Do not ask me not to grieve."

Aliah's lips turned into a smile that briefly lit her eyes with the vibrancy of life before the pain and shadows of death haunted their depths again. "I love you too, Duncan. I will watch over you both. Promise me to love our daughter enough for us both. Teach her my ways and yours. Make sure she is strong and brave like her father," she paused, and he nodded. He couldn't speak, his misery was lodged in his throat, choking him. "Now, I must finish this before I lose all of my strength. Turn away, my love."

"Never, I will stay here until the end, but I beg you to keep fighting, please." Duncan watched helplessly. He couldn't hold on to the person who breathed life into his lungs. His personal goddess he worshiped and clung to. Aliah pulled her hand away from his, and he knew, never again would he feel the warmth of her hand in his.

"Mother, please help me bring my daughter into this world and guide her to understand our ways."

"I will. I will, I love you, daughter."

"Then help me," Aliah begged. Duncan heard the plea laced in between her words. She wasn't just pleading for her mother to help bring their daughter into the world. She was begging her to help make it a better world for their daughter.

Aliah bent her knees and pushed. Her mother scrambled and moved between Aliah's legs to catch the baby. More blood rushed to the floor, painting the cave's stony ground red. Aliah kept pushing, but the baby wouldn't come.

Lilah encouraged her daughter to keep pushing, and that she was almost done, and to push just a little more.

Aliah pushed. Her eyes squeezed shut and clenched her jaw in pain from her efforts.

"I see her head! Sweetheart, push a little more," Lilah yelled excitedly at her daughter.

Aliah nodded, but her body was giving up. Duncan could tell by the way she let her head fall to the ground as if it weighed too much. Her arms fell next, limp by her sides. Duncan wanted to shout for her to keep pushing, but he didn't know if that meant she would be in more pain. Frustrated with his situation, he bent over and wiped the wisps of hair that stuck to her damp forehead.

"Come on, a little more, Aliah," he said and kissed her chilled lips.

Duncan watched as she pulled the last of her energy together for a final push. Then he heard it. He heard his daughter's cry and looked up to face Lilah. She stood unsteadily and walked toward them. Pride filled Lilah's eyes as she looked down at the bloodied bundle in her arms. She sat their baby on Aliah's chest. Aliah lifted her body and gave their daughter her first kiss. Tears ran down Aliah's face and dropped onto their daughter's face. The warm glow of new life settled on Lilah and Aliah's faces. Love flowed from them to the newborn and wrapped her in a blanket of protection until Asthmoth arrived and broke the enchantment.

His eyes narrowed in distrust, and his clenched jawline showed evidence of his teeth grinding. His lips thinned in a tight line of anger, and he struggled to find words. "Look at... it. This is no dragon. We are born dragon, not human. Look!"

Duncan looked down at Aliah, hoping she hadn't heard her father's hateful words, but Aliah's body was too far gone. She was focusing her entire being on holding their daughter as life quickly drained from her. Duncan picked up their daughter so she could relax. Once Duncan held her, Aliah's arms fell like heavyweights against the stone.

"Aquilla. Her name is Aquilla," she said.

Duncan nodded and rocked the wailing baby girl. He stayed as close as he could to his wife as he held Aquilla.

"Aquilla," he promised.

"Father."

"Yes, Aliah," he responded immediately. "Have you come to your senses? This child is an abomination. Look, she was born human."

Duncan braced himself to defend his family, but Queen Lilah beat him to it. She slapped the king's face.

"Now, is not the time for your ignorance and purist beliefs. Our daughter lays dying on the ground, and all you can think to do in her last minutes is to say, 'I told you so?' No, you will not do this in front of me. You will listen to her and do whatever she asks of you. Then you will tell her you love her. You two will not part in hate. I won't allow it."

The King looked at his wife for a long minute before he nodded and kneeled near Aliah's head.

Duncan kept rocking Aquilla, who continued wailing in his arms. Lilah came to take her, and he reluctantly let her go. Her grandmother cooed and rocked her while Duncan looked between his daughter and wife, lost in grief. But he would not leave Aliah alone with Asthmoth.

"Father, please do as Duncan suggested. I knew my death was a possibility, but I wanted this baby. I wanted a child with my mate, and I regret nothing. Now, it is time for you to put aside your notions of human versus dragon and try to unite both races so we can all survive the troublesome times to come. I know you love me, but I will not ask you to love my child. You can decide the relationship you will have with your granddaughter. Goodbye for now father, I will be with the Great Dragons now. My dying wish is for you to help my mate and all of you live on. Please help my mate, father."

Duncan watched as Aliah's eyes closed, and her body shimmered, shifting for the last time to her dragon. Her dragon roared. Her roar was deafening to his ears and echoed throughout the cave. The villagers outside heard. They'd quieted, but now, they were yelling and threatening his wife. Duncan placed a hand on her golden scales. He sobbed into her body. The rough texture of her scales prickled his face. He cried until he felt her body shiver and then, nothing. She had no more breaths to give. She was gone. Lilah kissed her daughter's long nose, tears poured from her eyes.

It wasn't until then he realized he wasn't the only one who lost today.

Asthmoth voice boomed. "We must act now. Duncan, take your daughter. Lilah stay next to me. We are leaving now! Aliah sacrificed herself for our lives. We will live on."

Asthmoth looked around. Grief clouded his eyes. He lifted his chin and yelled his battle cry, for himself, for his daughter, for their future, "For valor, we lift our fire with courage!"

They ran out of the cave and into the waiting mob.

Asthmoth yelled to the mob, "We killed it. We killed the dragon and got away!"

The mob crowded them, cheering their victory, and herding them to safety. Duncan held on to Aquilla, only letting her go to feed. There was a new mother in the mob who said she had milk to give. Duncan watched her feed Aquilla.

Once they made it to the camp they sat around the fire, discussing packing up and the next place they heard dragons were hiding.

After a while, Asthmoth sat next to him. Asthmoth followed Duncan's gaze.

"What will you and Lilah do next?"

"Lead your people away from mine."

Duncan nodded. "That's smart."

"Every land needs a leader; this one and humans are no different. I will teach you, humans, civility."

Duncan didn't know how he would manage it, but Asthmoth was a powerful force in his own right. He was someone you either fought or ran from. Duncan figured one reason they didn't get along was that Duncan didn't fit into either of those categories.

"My opinion of you and that monstrosity has not changed. My daughter asked me to save you and the baby, and so I did, but I want you and that thing to stay far away from my family and me. If I catch either of you near my wife or me, I will kill you and that child. She is only another human to me."

"If that is your choice, I will not fight you on it, and I will obey your wishes."

He and Asthmoth dropped into a charged silence. The fire crackled in front of them. The woman who fed Aquilla pushed her breasts back into her tunic and stood. She walked Aquilla to him and handed her to him. He took his daughter into his arms, and his world righted itself.

Asthmoth stood and looked down on them. "Remember my words," he said before striding away. He never looked back.

CHAPTER TWO

Duncan

"Father, tell me the story again."

"The story about Damascus and Priscilla?"

"Yes, that one."

Duncan reached down and mussed his daughter's thick brown hair. "No, it's bedtime, and all good little girls are already sleeping."

Aquilla pouted. "I'm a good girl," she said, then mumbled, "but I'm not sleeping."

"Then you aren't a good girl, are you?"

"I am," she said incredulously.

"Aquilla, I will tell you the story tomorrow night. We have a lot to do tomorrow, and if you plan on being my helper, then you will need lots and lots of rest."

"I will be your helper. You promised I could."

Duncan smiled. "And I meant it, but if you don't sleep, I don't know if I can let you be my helper tomorrow."

Aquilla tucked her head beneath her heavy covers. He heard her muffled voice say, "I'm already sleeping." She began snoring loudly.

Duncan laughed before he pulled her covers down to her chest. "Lift your arms."

She did then dropped them over the blankets. "Good, you are all tucked in. Now all you have to do is close your eyes. It's time to dream about princesses and princes, like all the other little girls."

"I won't dream about princesses. I want to dream about the finest sword ever made and the best battle ever fought!"

"Okay, but you can't fight in the battle, and you can't touch the sword, not even in your dreams."

"But I'm a big girl in my dreams."

"Okay, my little Lily, as long as you are a very, very big girl and you've learned how to use a sword."

Duncan scratched his chin and wondered how tucking his daughter into bed turned into a discussion about battles and swords? "Close your eyes, Aquilla."

She did. Duncan waited for a few minutes before leaving Aquilla's room. He walked into the living area of their small cabin and sat on his rocking chair. Duncan ran his hands over the smooth wood made from one of the smaller trees that surrounded their cabin this deep in the forest. He remembered when he made the rocking chair. Aquilla had been a tiny babe who wouldn't fall asleep unless she was in his arms. Duncan hadn't minded at all. He loved holding her close to him. Sometimes he felt if he didn't, she'd leave him like her mother. Grief pricked his heart anew at the thought of his wife.

Aliah would have loved it here.

Just like Aquilla loved it here. Not that she'd known any place other than here, and Duncan had no desire to introduce his sweet daughter to the evils of the world. He wanted her to live a carefree life. The sound of a light knock disrupted his thoughts. Duncan straightened and reached for his weapon. He stood with his sword firmly in hand and walked to the door.

Duncan lifted the door up and to the right. This time of the year, the wood swelled from the heat. When it opened wide, he bowed and moved aside to let the queen into his home.

"Is she asleep?" Queen Lilah asked.

"Yes, she fell asleep around a half an hour ago."

"Good, I brought her more clothes. I picked sensible clothes this time. Oh, and some shoes, so her little feet don't get a scar. Humans can scar, even from a simple cut. You must be careful," she said in a way that made Duncan believe she studied humans and determined they were fragile, and this recent revelation regarding her granddaughter's fragility frightened her.

Duncan nodded. "Thank you."

Lilah pushed past Duncan and walked straight to Aquilla's room. She stood over Aquilla's bed and watched her sleep. "I don't have long," she whispered hurriedly over her shoulder as she entered with Duncan close behind.

"You don't need to whisper. You could yell at the top of your lungs, and Aquilla wouldn't wake." His daughter was a deep sleeper. Sometimes she slept so deep Duncan worried for her. He'd mentioned it to Lilah during one of her visits. Lilah had only grinned at him and said, "It's a dragon thing." Her words did nothing to soothe him, but as time passed, Aquilla's deep sleeping went into his mind's bucket of unique things about Aquilla.

Lilah bent down and ran her hand through Aquilla's hair. She frowned. Aquilla's hair tangled around Lilah's fingers. Duncan grimaced. Lilah would yell at him again.

Carefully, Lilah untangled her fingers from Aquilla's hair. "I told you, you must brush her hair before she goes to sleep and when she wakes up. Otherwise, she will have knots, and her appearance will be more akin to a banshee than the granddaughter of a queen. This will not do, Duncan, and I've told you this before."

In his defense, Lilah had never tried to hold Aquilla down to brush her hair. Aquilla was as slippery as a snake and strong as an ox, which also went into his mind's bucket of things that were uniquely Aquilla, but still Duncan wanted to defend himself. "Lilah, I try, but she fights me like a madwoman. She's small, but she's stronger than she looks."

Lilah smothered a smile. "She is so like her mother. She also hated when I brushed her hair, but as she was a child and I was an adult, I won those fights." Lilah gave him a pointed look before moving past her reprimand. "Is she learning her letters?"

"Yes, she hates that as much as she hates for me to brush her hair."

"Well, if she ever wants to get one of those handsome, well-off human boys to notice her, she will learn her letters and brush her hair."

Duncan grimaced. "Boys? Over my dead body."

"Trust me. If Aquilla is like her mother, she will step over your dead body to go out with the boy of her choice."

The atmosphere changed from light to somber at the mention of Aliah. Lilah sighed. "In my granddaughter's five short years, I have never seen her eyes, and those eyes have never seen mine. I hate coming in the middle of the night and leaving without her ever knowing I was here or knowing that I exist. She is my daughter's legacy and being separated from her breaks my heart. She is so precious to me, one day she will know me."

Duncan remained silent. Speaking would only add to her pain. He knew her night visits directly defied her husband's commands. Every time he thought of what she risked to secretly see the granddaughter King Asthmoth called a monstrosity and a blight to his lineage, humbled him. She valued Aquilla more than the fallout that would come if Asthmoth ever found out she was stealing moments with her. Duncan glanced at Lilah and saw the sheen of unshed tears in her eyes as she stared down at Aquilla.

Quickly, Lilah stood and turned her back to him. She wiped the tears from her eyes and ran her shaking hands down her long purple silk dress, pressing out any wrinkles before turning to face him. By the time she did, her tears were dry, and her expression composed.

"My mate and King Athel of the Eastlands are fighting over where his border begins and where King Athel's ends again. He insists this time that if King Athel doesn't agree with him, there will be war, so if he goes to war, maybe I can have time during the day with Aquilla."

Duncan nodded. "Perhaps, but for your husband's sake, I hope there isn't a war, and for your sake, I hope there is."

"That's a strange contradiction, Duncan."

Duncan shrugged. He didn't want to crush her hopes by saying what was on the tip of his tongue. He wouldn't remind her of all the times war was on the horizon but never reached the gate.

Lilah turned toward Aquilla and lightly brushed the back of her hand against her cheek. "I must go. Keep my granddaughter safe."

"With my life," Duncan said.

Lilah nodded. With one last look at Aquilla, she turned and left Aquilla's room. Lilah didn't stop until she reached the door.

"Until next time, Duncan, be well."

"You too, my queen."

Lilah walked out, and Duncan followed behind her, stepping into the warm and humid night. She stopped. "Duncan, you have no queen, there's no need to make a fool of us both."

Duncan didn't deny it. He held no allegiance to anyone's Kingdom. If he had to fight, he would only fight to keep his daughter safe. Lilah disappeared into the forest. Duncan turned his head toward the skies, and within a moment after losing sight of her, he saw a large silhouette of a dragon streak through the sky. There wasn't a human alive who could see a dragon at night if the dragon didn't want to be seen, but Duncan, the mate of a dragon, was a little less human and a bit more dragon.

THE NEXT MORNING, DUNCAN heard Aquilla's voice before he saw her turn the corner. Every morning she said the same six words, and every morning, his pride swelled, grateful to the gods, they blessed him to be her father.

"Father, Father! Your daughter is awake."

Aquilla turned the corner with a wide smile. Then she jumped up with the full expectation he would catch her. He did, and he wrapped her within his arms and kissed the top of her head before he sat her down at the table.

Duncan turned to the counter and grabbed the bowl of porridge that he cooled for Aquilla. He sat her bowl in front of her, and she grabbed the wooden spoon and shoveled the porridge into her mouth.

"How is my favorite daughter this morning?"

Aquilla turned her nose up, her cute face marred with anger. "You have another daughter?"

Duncan tried but failed to hide his grin. "No, it was a joke."

"It wasn't funny," she said, pouting before she went back to giving her porridge her full attention.

Duncan shook his head and kissed her cheek. "I thought it was funny."

Aquilla spoke around a mouth full of porridge. "You always think your jokes are funny, even when I don't."

Duncan sat across from her and looked at his daughter. She was beautiful. She had so much of her mother's beauty. Then he looked at her hair and grimaced. It was obvious she hadn't bothered to brush it before she dressed. "Did you brush your hair today?"

She ignored him. It was something she'd begun doing lately when she didn't want to lie to him.

"Aquilla, did you brush your hair?"

She stopped eating and stared at him. Her hazel eyes bore into his soul. Sometimes Duncan thought he saw someone ancient staring back at him when he looked into the depths of his daughter's hazel eyes. Those were her mother's eyes, her mother's narrow nose and full lips. The only feature she'd had of his was her unruly hair.

"No, and I don't plan on it. My hair is fine."

Her hair was not fine. It stuck up in the back and tangled on the sides. Her hair was anything but fine. "Aquilla, after you finish eating, you will go back to your room and brush your hair."

"I hate brushing my hair, Father," she whined. "Please, don't make me do it."

Duncan held his hand up. "You are a young lady, and you must take care of your appearance."

Aquilla shook her head, vehemently disagreeing with him. "I'm a warrior. We aren't boy or girl, just brave."

Duncan lowered his hand and ran it down his face. Not for the first time, he wondered if he should have tried to teach her more womanly traits. Duncan never gave thought to his words. He said what he thought would work to get her to listen, which to his dismay, was the same thing he would say to a soldier. Duncan winced. She wasn't a soldier; she was his daughter.

"Well, warriors still brush their hair and polish their armor and weapons. Warriors take pride in their appearance."

"They do? Really?"

"Look at me. My hair is brushed, and I polish my sword every night."

Aquilla looked at him for a long time. Her expressions were windows to her thoughts. She was deciding if she wanted to believe him. Her features relaxed, and he knew she'd decided. Aquilla smiled brightly and nodded once.

"I will brush my hair. I want to be a polished warrior too."

"Or a pretty girl." Duncan quipped, and Aquilla frowned.

DUNCAN WASHED THE DISHES in a bucket of icy water he brought from the nearby stream. Aquilla was inside, brushing her hair. He could hear her screams of pain from where he stood outside.

"This is your own creation, Aquilla," Duncan said as he tried to convince himself not to run into the cabin and break the wretched brush in half.

Instead, Duncan went back to scrubbing the dishes using a bushel of pine. He heard another scream of pain from Aquilla. His fist clenched. Duncan sighed. Luckily, he finished the dishes before he rendered the bushel useless. He placed the bowls aside to dry before putting them away.

Duncan rubbed his wet hands down his tunic and sat on the stump he used to chop wood. His thoughts drifted to his daughter. He thought of a future where his daughter was a woman grown, talks of being a warrior dust in the wind, a phase she grew out of. He already mourned her innocence as she learned more about life, about people, and the gods help him, about boys. Perhaps, in a few years, she would tell him she wanted to sew or began taking over the cooking. Yes, Duncan thought, she would become interested in these things because these are things all women are born to do. They want to do them as much as they want to marry and have children.

No matter that Aquilla didn't have a mother, somehow her body would show her how to be a proper woman. He was sure of it. Eventually, she would become a woman on her own. For now, if she wanted to be a warrior, she could, and then when she changed her mind, he would encourage her.

Duncan felt better. There wasn't any harm in her playing as a child before she became a woman. He smiled at the thought of his wayward warrior following him around the forest and kicking her small legs up against an imagined foe. Duncan stood. He had a little warrior to retrieve. It was time for their day to begin.

IT HADN'T TAKEN AQUILLA long to finish brushing her hair after she got started. He gathered their things, and they left to hike the forest. As they walked, Aquilla couldn't stop talking. She asked him every question she could think of as soon as it came to her.

"Father, why must we walk so far into the forest to find good wood? There's wood right outside our house, why can't we use that?"

Duncan looked down at his daughter. Her face turned up to look at him as she waited for his answer. Aquilla's cherubic face was flush from their exertions, but she was doing great. Duncan smiled proudly. By the gods, he loved his child.

"If we use all the wood around our house, then how will we hide from our enemies? We need the trees to keep us covered, plus hiking every day, makes us strong."

"I want to be the strongest!" Aquilla yelled.

Duncan flinched. He didn't think being strong was something women should want.

AFTER A WHILE, THEY reached the clearing. Duncan sat their pack down. The breeze chilled his sweat-soaked back. Duncan ignored it and took a deep breath.

He opened his arms, soaking in everything the forest had to give. He enjoyed the feel of the sun on his skin. He inhaled the smells of the forest and felt the hard ground beneath his feet.

Aquilla walked to him. "Do we start now?"

Duncan shook his head. He sat next to her, pushing her feet off the pack. "No, now we rest from the long hike. Aren't you exhausted?"

She shook her head. "No, I'm not tired. I can keep going."

"I can't. I need to rest, and then we can begin. How about a snack while we catch our breath?"

"I want a snack," Aquilla exclaimed.

Duncan untied the rope that held the pack closed and he pulled out some dried deerskin and an apple. He handed them to her.

She took the dried meat and began gnawing at the edges, completely discarding the apple. Duncan picked up the apple and put it back into the pack for later. She would eat it once she ran out of meat.

Duncan sat back against the tree with Aquilla and ate his share. Looking out, he watched the clouds as they moved away from him. It was as if he was in a living painting. This far up in the mountain, it seemed like he could reach up and touch the clouds.

Duncan loved it all. Out here in the forest, he and Aquilla were far away from the intrigue of the palace. Far away from the horse carriages that filled the narrow walkways, the scandalous garments, and heavily perfumed women of wealth. Most importantly, they were far away from the king. Duncan didn't miss any of it. He didn't miss the desperate yells of the merchants out to sell wares to keep food on the table or the day drunkards who harassed men and women who had the misfortune of crossing their paths. No, the sounds, the look, and the feel of wild, untamed nature were far better.

Aquilla wasn't next to him when he looked down, thinking to try to convince her to eat her apple. He stood and looked around the tree where they rested. He found her there, stalking something in a bush. He watched her tilt her head to the left, then to the right. She hunched her back and braced herself on the balls of her feet. Then she leapt into the bush, fearless of the unknown. Duncan tensed, ready to protect her if she'd somehow stumbled upon something dangerous.

Relief flooded him when Aquilla's fox jumped out running away from her, but Aquilla was fast on the fox's heels. Usually, he would consider a fox dangerous, just not this fox. Aquilla and the fox in question had been inseparable from the time Duncan and Aquilla stumbled upon him in the forest, abandoned by his mother soon after birth. Duncan could only think that after his mother birthed him, a bigger predator came, and she ran, leaving her baby behind. When Aquilla saw the abandoned fox, she demanded they help it. She stood by the fox's side every day until they nursed him back to health, and every day since then, the fox found his way to their doorstep.

"Father, Fox is here! We will hunt rabbits for dinner."

Duncan shook his head. "No, we have food enough. We should only hunt when we need food and respect the lives of all the creatures in the world by only taking what we need and giving back when and what we can."

"Like when we planted the seeds for the new tree?" she asked.

"Yes, exactly like that. We have taken many trees. We should try to grow what we can, when we can."

"Okay," she said and rubbed her fox's belly. It was an odd sight. He'd never known a fox to want its belly rubbed.

"Are you ready to help me spar?"

Aquilla jumped up, then sank into a fighting stance, her tiny fists balled, and eyes determined. Duncan took that as a yes.

CHAPTER THREE

Aquilla

E **ight Years Later**
"Come on, old man, at the rate you're going it'll take nine hours to make it up the mountain. Come on with you," Aquilla shouted at her father behind her.

"If I were thirteen years old and made of energy, perhaps, I too could run through the mountain with your speed, but alas, I am almost two scores older than you!"

"Father, you can't fool me. Just yesterday you were running, jumping, and climbing through the mountain. Not to mention, we train every day."

"Go ahead. Leave me behind, and I will catch up soon." He shooed her along. "Go, Aquilla, go run all of your energy off, so you aren't circling me when we get home."

Aquilla smiled at her father and did as she was told. She ran through the forest, jumping over fallen trees, careful to watch her steps for hidden rabbit holes and vines that hid between the fallen leaves. Sweat dripped down her back, and her light linen top clung to her body, damp from her exertions. Her pants rubbed against her thighs, annoying her skin, but she ignored it and breathed in the fresh air. Being outside on a sunny day filled her with exhilaration and strength. Aquilla ducked under hanging branches and carefully avoided spider webs, so she did not disturb their home. When she grew closer to her destination, she slowed then halted at the sound of several men talking.

What are they doing here? Aquilla hid behind the closest tree with a thick trunk. She strained her ears to hear what they were saying, but she couldn't pick up anything more than the deep timbered murmurings of men. She gathered her courage and pushed down her curiosity before turning back toward her father. She had to warn him.

By the time Aquilla met up with her father, fear and anticipation left her breathless, too breathless to say anything to her father without taking a few deep breaths, first.

"Aquilla, are you showing off? That's poor sportsmanship, you know," her father said playfully.

Sweat dripped down the sides of her face, down to her chin before dropping to the ground. "Shh, Father, there are men ahead. I came back to warn you."

When her father's eyes met hers again, gone was the humor that she usually saw dancing within his green depths. Now they were cold, filled with steel and danger. He struggled out of the pack and let it drop to the ground. His hand went to his waist to secure his sword at his side. "Stay here, don't move an inch, and do not follow me. That's an order."

Aquilla opened her mouth to protest. She was fast and strong. She could help him, but she said nothing. When her father gave an order, he meant for her to follow it. Aquilla kicked a pinecone on the ground. She was crestfallen but understood the way of things. She watched her father go, leaving her defenseless next to a tree without a sword. Not for the first time, Aquilla cursed her father for not letting her bring her sword to practice. It was of no use to anyone sitting in her room collecting dust.

She shook her head. She had to stay alert and focused, ready to respond to any threat or help her father when he called for her. Aquilla stood with her eyes closed in concentration. Seeing wasn't what mattered this far in the forest where everything was good at hiding. Listening was. Aquilla listened for the sound of a breaking branch on the forest floor. The rustle of leaves under someone's feet as they walked or ran forward. No one could move without making noise unless they could fly.

Soon she heard movement. She tilted her head to the left then right, pinpointing the direction before opening her eyes.

Someone was coming. Aquilla balled her hands into fists and dropped into a fighting stance. She may not have her sword, but she still had her fists.

As she waited and listened for her target to approach, a thrill of adrenaline coursed through her. Soon, her father appeared from the brush, disheveled and out of breath.

"Aquilla, grab the pack, and let's go home. It appears the nobles are hunting today. We can't be spotted. As a matter of fact, it's best if we stay inside the cabin for the next few days. Come. Quickly, Aquilla," her father demanded.

Aquilla nodded, picked up their pack, and walked ahead of her father, wondering why his eyes held unmistakable fear.

IT WAS ONE DAY AFTER she'd heard the men in the forest and Aquilla hadn't been outside. She flopped down onto her bed. Her body was full of restless energy. It was already noon, and the day was dwindling. Her body yearned to run through the forest, practice, and play with Fox.

Aquilla tossed on her bed, careful not to throw herself around too much. She'd grown over the years, and her bed wasn't as steady as it once was. Father said a year ago he would make her a new bed, with white oak, one that he said would be a bed 'fit for a princess.' Aquilla didn't care about a pretty bed. She just wanted a sturdy bed long enough to fit her from head to toe.

She looked longingly toward the window. Father wouldn't be very upset if she went outside but stayed close to the cabin. She wouldn't go too far, just far enough that her father wouldn't hear her if she and Fox were loud, and she knew just the place. Aquilla sat up and pulled her shoes on. Adventure awaited.

And so will punishment if I get caught.

She banished the thought and sneaked out of the house.

CHAPTER FOUR

Garret

Prince Garret slipped away from his father and their entourage. He'd been edging further and further away from his father, who was fast losing his game of word sparring with King Asthmoth. That was the way of things with dragons like them. Neither wanted to be beaten by the other in accomplishments and wealth—land and humans included.

Garret didn't see the big deal. Why couldn't the two kings get along if both lands were in a state of peace?

Garret moved farther away from his father and King Asthmoth until they were out of sight. Then he looked for something big to hunt. He was fifteen years old now. Hunting minor game like birds and rabbits were for babies. Men ruled kingdoms at his age, or so his father reminded him.

Garret walked, careful not to turn himself around, and end up in the sights of his father's hunting party. He was listening for his prey when he heard a girl.

"Fox, Fox, where are you? Come here, you clever fox. I saw you looking for me from my window. I'm here now, so come out. I want to play."

Garret's curiosity pushed him to see what type of girl would dare to run unaccompanied through the forest looking for foxes. He'd never seen the like. He had to find out. Garret walked toward the sound of her voice, careful not to make a sound.

"I can hear you, Fox," she taunted.

Garret inhaled. He didn't smell a fox nearby, nor did he see one. Those were his last thoughts before he found himself flat on his back, taken unawares. Garret felt the sharp pain from the rock pushing into his spine. He would have bruises tomorrow, if not yet this evening.

"Got you!" she said, pinning him down by his shoulders.

Garret bucked beneath her, but she held him steady. She was strong for a girl. "Get off me, you imbecile. I'm no fox!"

She rolled over, then bounced up and sank into a perfect fighting stance.

Who is this girl? Judging by the look in her eyes, she was less than one minute from attempting to thrash him. Garret held his hand up. "Halt. Do not move. I was in the area, and I heard you while I was hunting. I mean you no harm."

She stared at him with her wild and familiar hazel eyes. He wondered if she'd ask him where his hunting bow was? Garret hadn't needed one. He'd planned to use his claws. Behind her he heard a low, menacing growl. Garret's breath stopped. He used the hand that he held in the air to point behind her. He was sure she could hear the beast that lurked behind her as he could. But the girl didn't move. The fox growled at them again, this time showing teeth and black gums. If he were alone, he would have growled back and shown his teeth, but he couldn't do that with a human watching.

"I think we should run, like right now."

Garret braced himself for the worst when the fox was close enough to the girl to tear her spleen out with its teeth. She had to know it, but she didn't move. Was she so afraid that she couldn't move? Should he take control of the situation? But how could he do that if he couldn't shift into a dragon?

Thoughts, words, breath, and several other senses were knocked from him when the girl exploded and tackled the dangerous fox. Garret bounced on the balls of his feet ready to jump in and save her from the beast, but then he noticed the fox wasn't ripping her to shreds. He carefully nipped her here and there as they rolled around trying to pin each other. Garret couldn't believe his eyes.

What is she, an animal whisperer? He'd heard of such humans who could tame lions and bears with a look, but he'd never seen it. *Until now.*

After watching the two for a handful of heart-clenching minutes, the fox pinned her down and growled in her face. Once again, Garret braced himself to protect her. Then the fox licked her face. Would wonder ever cease with this girl? Fed up with the two of them, Garret shifted his weight to turn and walk away from the pair. Then he heard her laughter. Her laughter was innocence and wine. The greatest opera he'd ever heard sung by the best voice in all the land.

She stood and waved her arms in front of him. He shook himself out of his haze.

"Hello, my name is Aquilla. What's yours?" Her English was perfect. She didn't speak in the garbled mix and mash of old Celtic and English the commoners spoke.

"I'm-I'm, Garret, how do you do?" He asked, sputtering through his introduction.

She smiled. "Fine, and this guy," she said and pointed down to the fox. "Is Fox. I've known him since he was a pup."

That took away some of his awe of her. Who named a fox, Fox?

She went on. "There's not much to do in these woods aside from hunting and cutting trees. Fox and I sometimes hunt together. We don't kill what we catch most of the time unless we need to eat. If you want to play with us, I suppose that's okay. We've never seen another person before that wasn't family."

"Truly?" Garret said and stood a little taller. She'd lucked out and ran across a prince as her first nonrelative. He opened his mouth to say his full royal title then shut it as she and Fox ran away.

"Come on!" she yelled, and just like that, he followed her.

THE THREE OF THEM PLAYED for what felt like years. He felt free and at peace with this strange human. Were they all like her? Father said they were vile, but she wasn't. She was lovely, captivating, and kind. Maybe he'd misjudged the humans, or perhaps his father was wrong.

"Jump when we tell you to, or you won't make it over the next part, okay?" Aquilla yelled to him, bringing him back to the forest and the game they were playing.

"Okay!" he yelled to her back.

"Here we go, pick up speed now!"

Garret smiled. Pick up speed? That he could do. Grinning, he passed her. She pointed ahead. That's when he saw the cliff in front of them. They would have to jump it or go around. It was clear from Aquilla's pace behind him; she intended to jump. He could cover the distance with ease, but he worried about Aquilla. He reached the cliff and bent his knees before springing off. On the other side, his feet hit the hard dirt then he tucked and rolled. Quickly, he turned around, concern for Aquilla seizing his heart. No human woman he'd ever met could cover the distance with ease. He tensed, ready to shift into his dragon form to catch her if he had to. He'd do anything but let her fall.

She hit the cliff and jumped. Straight behind her was Fox. She landed next to Garret, rolled, and took off running.

Does she ever tire?

Garret shook his head, smiled, then took off after her. It didn't matter if she didn't. He could keep up with her. Ten minutes later, she stopped and looked behind her. He stopped too and waved.

Yes, Human, I can keep up with you.

"Come here. We made it to my favorite place in the whole forest. Next time your father brings you here and Fox and I aren't around, come here and wait for him. See, it's pretty and has food to nibble on while you wait."

She jumped up and grabbed an apple from a tree, then settled in front of a bright blue stream. Garret had to admit, the place was beautiful. He sat down beside her. He could see fish of every color swimming in the clear blue water.

"How did you find this place?" he asked.

"I like to explore with Fox. We have a lot of time on our hands."

"Do you live on the mountain?"

"Yes," she said in a way that implied he shouldn't ask any more questions, so he wouldn't.

"Do you think we should go back soon?" he asked.

Garret watched her lift her head to the sky and sigh heavily.

"Perhaps, we can take a shortcut back." Then, amazingly, she winked at him.

Garret gaped. Never in all his years had he been on the receiving end of a wink. He didn't know how he felt about it, but he didn't have time to think, because once again, Aquilla was off.

A FEW MINUTES LATER, they were back where they started. The best thing about the way she led him back was that it didn't include jumping off a cliff. Garret wondered why they took the harder path to begin with. He asked her as much.

"Because the long way is fun, right?" she said.

Garret couldn't disagree. Shortly after they arrived, he heard Wulf calling his name.

"Prince Garret! Prince Garret!"

Garret turned toward her, prepared to launch into a plethora of reasons why he hadn't told her who he was, only to find Aquilla gone. She'd been standing right there, and now she wasn't. He turned in a full circle, looking for any trace of her and Fox, but she and Fox were gone. It was like she disappeared.

"Down here!" Garret called to Wulf, the man recently appointed his bodyguard, to Wulf's great dislike.

"Where is my father?" Garret asked.

"Not far, my Prince. He has started the journey back to King Asthmoth's castle. I will accompany you now. We have horses waiting for us at the top of the hill."

Garret nodded, and they began walking up the hill, Garret trailed behind, hoping to catch a glance of Aquilla before he left. He left disappointed; he didn't see her and likely never would again.

When Garret reached his horse, he untied it from the tree. Wulf patted his shoulder, and Garret eyed him suspiciously. Why was he being nice? On a normal day, he'd not hear more than the occasional 'Yes, my Prince or No, my Prince.' Garret mounted his horse, King Charles, and commanded him to trot.

CHAPTER FIVE

Lilah

Her dream started with memories of her childhood. She remembered how happy she was the time her father told her the story of Damascus and Priscilla. Then, her dream twisted, she stood in a cold dark place she'd never been before. The rough texture of the ground stuck to her soles like sand.

She couldn't see anything. The darkness was impenetrable, even with her heightened senses from her dragon. Lilah saw something move to her right. She spun looking for what she'd seen, but there was nothing there except more darkness. Lilah took several steps back. Something stalked her, a predator far greater than she or her dragon. Her body shook with fear. Something watched her, something vile and evil. Without thinking, she turned and ran.

A horrifying laugh echoed around her as if its laugh had its own life, its own evil. She kept running.

"Wake up, Lilah, wake up." She told herself to be afraid, but she didn't wake. When she turned to look over her shoulder, she saw two large glowing green eyes pierce the darkness, moving, chasing her. Lilah pulled at her dragon, but she couldn't shift. Her fear struck her to her core.

It roared, a frightening sound. She stopped and crouched down, hands over her ears as the roar bounced around her.

"What do you want for me?" Lilah yelled. Tears fell fast down her face.

"I want Her," it responded. Lilah screamed when she felt its fiery breath on the back of her neck, searing her skin like acid.

"Who is she?" Lilah cried. She would say or do anything to get away from it.

"She is the sun. She is light within a world of darkness. She is the only thing that keeps me from my rightful place. She slept for a very long time, but I feel her, I feel her like ants crawling up and down my body. Now is the time. She's there, you know, and, she's mortal and killable." The voice laughed with manic delight.

Lilah stayed crouched on the ground, hands covering her ears, chin resting on her knees. None of this had anything to do with her. She wanted to wake up.

"You have made a mistake. This has nothing to do with me," she said.

"Yes, it does," the creature hissed. "I know your secret, Queen Lilah. I know your heart is growing dark. You hate your mate for not letting you see your granddaughter. You hate him for disowning your daughter. You hate him for keeping you away from her, and now dear queen, she's gone, and you hate him more for that."

"I don't. No, I don't!" Lilah cried, but she knew he was right. She hated her mate. She hated him more and more every day.

"No, do not lie to me. I am darkness. I recognize myself in you. Don't fret. You can have everything you desire. I know it because I can see the future and what's coming will surely kill him. Think of it as a gift."

Lilah worried her bottom lip. "What do you want for this gift?"

"Nothing. Just a promise. Very simple. Nothing you haven't done before. In exchange, I will tell you how to stay alive so you can see your precious granddaughter, but if you don't promise, I'll see you dead with your worthless mate."

"What do you want me to do?"

"A tiny thing. Kill Her when you see Her."

"I can't just kill someone for being Her without knowing if she deserves to die.

It yelled. "You do not ask me questions. You do not tell me no. You don't have any power here."

"I'm sorry. I'm sorry. Please, just don't kill me. I want to live. I have my granddaughter to take care of."

Lilah thought it left. Her stomach turned with nervousness and relief, but what if this thing weren't a nightmare from the depths of her black soul, but a being that could help her?

"Please, don't leave me. Please, I'll do whatever you want, tell me what to do," Lilah pleaded.

"Then do you agree?"

"Yes, but what happens if I can't do it?"

"Then I become flesh too."

"What does that mean?"

"Nothing, for you to worry about. It means if you can't kill Her, I will help you along. Wouldn't that be nice? If you couldn't finish the job, you could close your eyes and let me do it? Then all will be well."

"If you could do it, then why not now?" Lilah dared to ask.

"I need you, dear queen or more precisely, I need your body. I can do the killing, while you will be something like a passenger in your body you could even...play dead if you wanted, so you'd miss the entire messy business. Then when I'm done, we both return to where we belong. It's a win-win for you if you ask me."

Lilah chewed the inside of her cheek in thought. "Okay, and you will tell me how to survive my... gift."

"Surely. I will do so tonight before you wake. You have my word. So, do we have a deal?"

"Yes," she said, shocked at the ease at which she could sign her mate's life over to Hades.

CHAPTER SIX

Aquilla

As Aquilla approached the cabin, she heard the muted sound of a blade hitting wood. Her father must be outside chopping. Aquilla didn't bother going through her window. She wasn't a coward. She would take her punishment as a warrior would, but that didn't mean she had to look forward to it. Aquilla pushed her hand through Fox's fur. The coarse locks of his reddish-orange fur and the warmth of his body grounded her. She had a glorious day with Fox and Garret, and it was worth the punishment she would get. Aquilla took a deep breath and approached her father.

"Father, would you like me to finish chopping the wood?" she asked.

He ignored her and lifted the ax then swung it down with incredible force splitting the wood in two. Aquilla watched as he bent and picked up another log and split that one in two. He brought his blade down once, twice, thrice times before he turned toward her.

His nostrils flared and his cheeks were mottled with red from anger or exertion, maybe both. "Where were you, Aquilla?"

"I went to play with Fox," she didn't think now was the time to tell him about Garret. She wasn't lying exactly, she just omitted parts of her day.

"After I told you to stay indoors?"

"Yes," she said.

"Why? Why did you do it?"

"Because I felt like my body would split into two if I didn't go out-side. I tried Father, I really did, but I could not stay inside another minute."

Her father stared at her. Aquilla straightened and lifted her chin under his glare. She was wrong, so she would be punished; that was the way of things. She wouldn't try to run from it.

"You will chop wood for a week three times a day. Also, you will add one hundred sword strokes to your practice routine, and thirty minutes of running both in the morning and at night."

Not too bad. Things could have been worse. He could have told her she couldn't go outside for a week, and that may have killed her.

"Yes, Father."

"You're a thirteen year old girl who is growing into a woman. You don't know the dangers for women, but I do, so if I give you instruction, it is to keep you safe. If you must disobey me, do so by not listening when you are learning your letters, or not finishing your chores, but do not disobey me when I tell you not to leave the house. Ever. Do you un-derstand?"

Aquilla nodded, but she wasn't sure she could keep her word. She had to be outside. She just had to be.

Her father picked up another log and waved her away. "Now, get cleaned up. Dinner is ready. Fox, you go home."

Fox licked her hand then took off into the woods toward home. Aquilla hoped he didn't get in trouble by his den mother. Did fox's par-ents order him around as her father ordered her? Fox could probably run as free and as long as he liked as long as he returned home to sleep. Aquilla yearned for freedom to run until she felt like she was flying. Her father wouldn't understand. He didn't understand most things she felt.

CHAPTER SEVEN

Duncan

L ater that night, Duncan sat on his chair, reliving the fear and utter despair he felt when he entered Aquilla's room and she wasn't there. He tried to follow her trail, but when she was with Fox, he always used his tail to cover their tracks. He came close enough to the two kings he heard bits and pieces of their strained conversation.

If war was on the horizon eight years ago, it was knocking at the door now, and his daughter, the only person in the world he cared for, was somewhere amongst those dragons. He didn't want to think about what could have happened if she crossed paths with King Asthmoth. He'd made it clear what he thought about his daughter when she was born.

A knock startled him. He stood from his rocking chair and picked up his sword. He opened the door to find Lilah standing in front of him.

"Hello, Duncan, is she asleep?" she asked.

"She is."

Lilah nodded, and her eyes dimmed with disappointment. She sat on Aquilla's rocking chair. Duncan stopped his eyes from rolling in frustration. Whenever Lilah sat down, it was to talk because she had something to say about his parenting. Instead of showing his frustration, he rested his sword against the side of the fireplace and threw in a log. He poked the fire back to life several times before sitting.

"I thought tonight I should speak with you about something my granddaughter will experience soon"

"What?" Duncan asked.

Lilah continued, "Soon, she will begin her monthlies, and her upper body will change. Since you insist on living so far from other humans, you will need to help her through this. I have tried to think of everything you will need to prepare you for what's to come. I left a package on the porch for you to deal with. She will need the herbs to help with stomach cramps that may overcome her during this time."

Duncan watched Lilah stare at the crackling fire. Her body was here but her mind seemed far away. Before Duncan had the chance to ask her what was wrong, she stood. "I will leave this to you. I will not trouble my granddaughter this night. Until next time Duncan, be safe."

"You too, Lilah, and thank you for thinking of Aquilla."

"No matter what my husband thinks that girl is one of mine."

Duncan smiled. "She is."

AFTER WALKING LILAH out, Duncan sat down in front of the fire alone. He laid his head against the back of his chair and rocked. As he rocked, he thought of his daughter when she was a baby, how he worried about her not getting enough milk, or sleeping too much. Duncan hadn't known what was normal and what wasn't for babies. He remembered how he played with her toes, and she giggled in the innocent ways only babies could. Today when she snuck away from him, his heart stopped and stuck in his throat, his worry and fear trapped him.

He was helpless, and thoughts of the worst situations ran through his mind, making him crazy with pent up frustration and despair. Duncan wanted to protect her from everything, from scrapes on her little knees to the pain of brushing tangled hair. There was nothing Duncan wouldn't do for his daughter. She was the last remaining remnant of his beloved wife and the manifestation of the love between them. He couldn't lose her.

He closed his eyes and smiled as images of the last thirteen years with his daughter played behind his eyes before he drifted to sleep.

CHAPTER EIGHT

Aquilla

Aquilla woke to a scratching sound outside of her window. She smiled before she hoisted herself from her bed. Her bare feet touched the ground. She yelped as the chill of the floor ran up her legs, leaving goose bumps in its wake. She jumped back into her bed and felt around for the wool socks her father bought for her on one of his few trips to town.

"Found you," she said and lifted them in the air. "How do you get off my feet every night?"

Her feet were wrapped snuggly inside her socks again, so this time when she jumped off the bed she ran to her window. She looked around until she spotted Fox, the scratching culprit.

Aquilla looked up to the sky. The position of the sun told her it was still early.

"Why so early?" she asked and waited for an answer she knew would never come. Nevertheless, she always talked to Fox as if he were just as human as she was, and sometimes, she thought he was.

After receiving a look from Fox that included his tongue hanging from one side. Aquilla smiled down at him. "Okay, I have to chop wood anyway, I will be right out. Wait for me in the back."

Fox gave her one last look that said, "hurry up," before he bounded to the back of the house. Aquilla smiled and slipped off her favorite, red bed shirt and walked to the opposite side of her small room and washed using the warm water her father heated and sat in her room while she slept.

"Ouch!" Aquilla said as she washed her chest. Her chest had been tender as if bruised for weeks, but she couldn't figure out how she hurt herself. The swelling worried her. She poked at the two swollen areas on her chest and sucked in a breath against the tenderness. She inhaled deeply. Aquilla didn't want to tell her father she might need to see a healer. He never took it well when she hurt herself, even though she always healed fast, except for now.

"I will give it another day, and if it doesn't get better, I will tell Father."

Aquilla nodded her head, feeling comforted that she had a plan and continued dressing.

Finished dressing and prodding her injuries, she slipped into shoes and skipped toward the kitchen.

"Good morning!" she said before pressing against her father in a tight embrace. She squeezed too tight and hissed from the pain of her bruised chest. Aquilla let go of her father, hoping he hadn't realized she hurt herself. When she looked at her father, she knew he had. He frowned and several deep horizontal wrinkles of worry appeared across his forehead. He looked down her body to locate the source of her pain.

"Is something wrong?" he asked.

Aquilla lifted a hand to the back of her neck and rubbed as she tried to think of a way to explain things to her father without setting him off in a fit. There was nothing she could do but say it honestly.

"I must have fallen on my chest or bumped it against something because there's some swelling that won't go down. When I wash my chest, it hurts like a bruise, but I can't remember how I could have gotten the bruises."

Her father let out an exaggerated sigh and wiped one of his large callused hands down his face. She could hear the friction of his calloused hand rubbing against his beard.

"Sit." He pointed to a seat at the table where a bowl of steaming porridge sat. "We need to discuss this."

She sat and picked up the wooden spoon and shoveled large spoonful's of porridge into her mouth. She regretted being so greedy and not letting the porridge cool properly. She moved the hot oats around in her mouth as she waited for her father to say whatever he had to say. She hoped he wouldn't be long, remembering that Fox was in the back waiting for her. If she didn't get out there soon, he would get into a lot of trouble. His tendency to eat the meat they stored in the shed was something of legend, and every time her father threatened to replace the meat with him.

"What do you want to talk about, Father?"

He cleared his throat. "Men and women are different. Not just because your hair is long and mine is short, but in the way, our bodies develop."

Aquilla nodded. She knew men and women were different. It was as obvious as a fox differing from a wolf, or a bear from a fish.

"Well, women have babies, like Fox's mom had him." Aquilla nodded, and her father continued. "Well, to feed Fox, she needed special, um, bottles...no." He shook his head. "That's not right. I don't know how to say this. Let me try again. Fox's mother feed him using her b-breasts."

"What are breasts?" she asked and shoveled the last scoop of porridge into her mouth.

"Right, I knew you would ask that. Okay, let's see, a woman's breasts grow from her chest so she can feed her babes."

Aquilla nodded. "Where are breasts?"

"Should have seen that coming. They are on your chest." Her father began patting his chest. Aquilla looked down at her chest, which was swollen but nothing like her father's.

"Your breasts are bigger than mine," she said.

"No, no, Aquilla, your breasts won't be like mine. Yours will be bigger, okay, nevermind, just know, your chest will grow, and that is normal, and it will hurt a bit, I'd imagine."

"For how long?" Aquilla asked.

"For how long what?"

"How long will my chest hurt?"

"Not long, or maybe a little while. I'm not sure. Later I will show you how to protect your chest, so it won't irritate you when if you brush against something."

"Great." Aquilla stood. "I'm off to do my chores. Fox is waiting. I love you, Father, and I am sorry for leaving after you told me not to."

Her father smiled and waved a hand at her, shooing her outside.

CHAPTER NINE

Garret

His father dropped onto a chair, threw his feet on the table, and frowned. "What a waste of time. I hate sharing the same air as King Asthmoth with his high and mighty attitude, it just rankles me that he thinks so highly of himself."

Garret sat on a chair in the corner far away from his father. He played with the black marble he kept in his pocket. The marble reminded him to watch himself. He had to be blank, smooth, unblemished, dark without light, aloof. He had to be unreadable to those who wanted to know what he was thinking so they couldn't use him. Every royal knew a crown prince had to walk a delicate balance. Too much ambition and his father would fear that Garret would try to overthrow him, and too little and he became useless. Garret had figured out the perfect balance to appease his father. He wasn't too much one way or the other.

"Calm yourself, King Athel, we have what we need, what we came here for, so all was not a waste," said Alistair, his adviser, and personal witch. He was a vile creature, Garret thought, not for the first time. There were times it seemed his father's unreasonable behavior was because of Alistair's wicked influence.

Garret fought not to raise his head and glare at him.

"Yes, we did, didn't we," his father said thoughtfully. Then whispered so low, not even a passing dragon could hear. "When we come to take this kingdom, we will come through the forest. Wulf told me he marked the easiest points of entry while he searched for my wayward son, who did as he always does on hunts, disappear. Thank you for being so predictable and for giving us an excuse to wander through Asthmoth's kingdom, boy."

Garret could barely stop his eyes from rolling, but he prevented the telling emotion from appearing on his face. He would play his role. He would be blank, like the marble in his pocket.

He didn't regret the time he spent in the forest with Aquilla. His time with her and Fox gave him the courage to find out more about humans. He'd talked to several since returning to Asthmoth's castle. They all seemed nice once they got past his title. His father was wrong about the way he treated and spoke of humans. They were fragile, but they had value and deserved their protection.

GARRET PRETENDED NOT to listen as Alistair and his father spoke of court matters. If he were to be king, he'd need to understand how to run a kingdom. His father refused to talk to him about kingdom matters, happy to leave him in the dark, but Garret listened and watched. He knew far more than his father believed.

Garret listened as they discussed the humans who were starving in Inhous because of a sudden drought. Alistair advised his father against helping the humans because they could find something to do. Even Garret knew after starvation comes disease. If they didn't help them, then the humans would only become diseased and die. The dragons may be immune, but not the other humans. They had to do something.

"Alistair, you are right. If you don't work, you don't eat. The commoners who starve are simply lazy. I shouldn't take from my horde, I mean, coffers for them. If I do, they will never help themselves again.

They would just call on me and ask me to solve all their problems, and that won't do," His father said rather ignorantly.

He couldn't stand it a moment longer. What if Aquilla was one of the humans in his kingdom who needed his help? He couldn't live with himself if he'd caused her harm. The humans who were starving in his kingdom took on Aquilla's face. Her hazel eyes and brown hair tied up in a topknot, and her laughter and smile, but most of all, her innocence. The thought of her lying somewhere dying when she could be helped was too much for him to bear. He felt suffocated by his father and Alistair's presence. He had to get out.

"Father, I need to relieve myself."

"Go boy and be ready to leave early tomorrow, and I don't want to return to this castle until my banner hangs over it."

Garret bowed and spun on his heels. He couldn't get away fast enough. Garret heard Wulf's footsteps right behind him. As soon as the door to his father's room closed behind him, he unbuttoned the top two buttons of his white, high-neck silk blouse.

Garret jumped at the feel of a firm grip on his shoulder. He turned around to see Wulf. "Calm down Garret, don't let anyone see your emotions. Remember this young prince. We may be dark ones, but that doesn't make us murderers."

For the second time in as many days, Wulf spoke over two words to him. What was really strange was how proud Garret felt to know that Wulf, the greatest of their dragon warriors, saw something inside of him worth breaking his usual silence. Having this small gift made Garret feel proud.

Garret nodded and walked toward his room. He thought over Wulf's words. No, they didn't have to be murderers and deny aid to the humans when they had more than enough to give. It was condemning them to death, and they didn't deserve it. Absently, he waved to two noble girls who waved and giggled back. He nearly rolled his eyes. All they were good for was gossiping and giggling. If he married his queen, she would have to be brave and strong enough to shoulder his burdens with him. He didn't want to marry a dim-witted girl with white lace gloves and golden locks that shone like the sun.

An image of hazel eyes full of mischief and life flashed in his mind. He smiled to himself at the thought of her and how a chance meeting would change him forever, and he liked it.

CHAPTER TEN

Aquilla

Five Years Later

After a successful day of hunting and training, Aquilla and her father returned home with three hares for dinner and a deer to skin and store for the winter. Aquilla thought about using the deerskin to try making her father a new pack. She wanted to learn how to sew better, but it was boring. She didn't enjoy sitting for hours, moving a needle up and down. Most of the time, her stitches weren't straight, and she'd have to start again or leave them, which she was prone to do.

Lost in her thoughts, she hadn't realized how long she'd been silent until she heard her father ask her, "Are you feeling well?"

"Yes, I was just thinking about making something from the deerskin."

He looked at her skeptically. "I'd hate to waste it, Aquilla."

She wanted to protest, but she knew if he took the deerskin to the market, he could get some coins for it, which would be better than what she'd do with it.

"You're probably right. Maybe another time."

"Some other time. Your sword fighting has improved much, daughter."

"Shouldn't it? We train every day." Aquilla said smiling widely at her father.

"Yes, and if I were to let you 'zone out' as you say, I'm sure you would beat me one hundred times."

That was true. Aquilla didn't know what happened to her when she zoned out. She became someone else entirely. Her senses heightened, and everything around her slowed down. It was easy for her to anticipate her opponent's next strike and block it. Her mind was blank, and her body reacted. She was dangerous in those times. She'd almost hurt her father once. After that, he'd warned her never to zone out while she sparred.

"Yes, but that's because you trained me so well."

"You know, I don't know what happens when you zone out, but if there ever comes a time where you are facing an enemy, do any and everything to survive. Zone out, kick, bite, nothing is off the table."

His words shocked Aquilla. "Father that is dishonorable."

"No daughter, there's only one rule when you are fighting my sweet Lily, and that is to survive, by any means necessary."

He reached up to her cheek and patted it softly. "More than anything, I want you to survive."

Aquilla grabbed her father's hand and squeezed. "I will." She tried walking around him, but he grabbed her arm.

"I mean it. If something were to happen to me, I need you to know that I want you to survive. I want you to live on and be happy. Do not despair or feel guilt for surviving if I cannot. Do you understand?"

Aquilla was silent. Why would there ever be a time he'd be in danger, and she wasn't around to protect him?

"I understand," Aquilla said.

"Good. Let's keep moving."

THEY MADE IT BACK TO the cabin in less than an hour.

Her father hung the deer in the back to take care of later, but she knew she could skin the deer just as well as her father.

"I can do it, Father. I know how."

"Women shouldn't do such things, Aquilla. One day you will want to marry, and what will you list as traits for your future husband? Sword fighting, hand to hand combat skills, ability to not sew, lack of desire to comb or wash her hair, the ability to hunt, skin and cook a deer single handily. Aquilla, I want grandchildren one day."

Aquilla rolled her eyes. He sounded like she did when she begged for thirds. His recent talk of marrying and grandchildren annoyed her. She wasn't interested in marrying. She only wanted to fight to be the strongest. She wanted to defeat evil and protect the weak.

Something darted between the trees in front of their cabin.

"Fox?"

He peeked his head out first from behind a tree then the rest of his body appeared. He was a large fox. Standing, he came to her waist. He slunk closer to the shed where the deer hung.

"Hey, don't you go near Father's deer." She pointed her finger at him and frowned. "I mean it, Fox."

Fox looked between her and the deer twice before he decided not to test her resolve. Aquilla's father said more than once he didn't think Fox was a fox. When she asked him what Fox was, he didn't have an answer, so she decided until her father figured out what Fox was, he'd be a fox. More accurately, he was her fox.

She wondered if Fox's mother bothered him about mating. Then it occurred to her Fox might already have a mate and pups. Aquilla bent down and pulled his nuzzle to her face.

"Do you have pups and a mate waiting on you every day while you play with me?"

Fox whined. He must have thought he was in trouble; she let him go, but she didn't back away. Fox licked her face.

"Oh, nasty. I don't know what you did with your mouth today."

She grabbed his neck and wrapped her arm around it, then pushed him over. They fell, tumbling around each other.

"So, I should add taming a wild beast to the list of desirable marriage characteristics," her father said from behind her.

Aquilla popped up. "First, Fox is family, not a wild beast. Second, he's far from tame."

Her father smiled. "Go wash at the stream. You stink, and so does Fox."

Aquilla nodded, rushed in the cabin, grabbed her items to wash, then ran out of the cabin with Fox on her heels.

AQUILLA SAT AT THE stream, lying flat on her back, looking up at the clouds as they rolled by. Aquilla would get around to washing, but she wanted to take some time to sit and name the clouds with Fox's head resting on her stomach, where she idly ran her hand through his fur.

After a while, Aquilla walked into the water that was so icy it chilled her to the bone. She was sure she'd washed faster than ever before because the water seemed colder. Even colder than it was when they'd recently passed. She moved to walk out of the water, but Fox barked at her. She knew why.

"Fine, fine! I will wash my stupid hair. I don't know why Father won't let me cut it. If I cut it, then I don't have to keep arguing with him about brushing it at night."

Fox's only reply was to bark again, and for good measure, he added a growl. Aquilla rolled her eyes, then reached and pulled the leather strap from her topknot. Her long, thick brown hair hung down to the middle of her back.

"Happy now?" Aquilla asked Fox.

He did that tongue hanging thing she'd begun taking as Fox's way of saying, yes.

Feeling refreshed, Aquilla began her journey back home. On the way, she sang and picked flowers to give to her father. Her spirits were high.

CHAPTER ELEVEN

Garret

Seven days ago, his father decided to siege Asthmoth's castle. Three days ago, they set out to take Asthmoth's land by force and trickery. In his tent, he sat at the table as the sounds of the night surrounded him. He heard the call of the crickets as the night creatures roused from their day slumber. Usually, the night brought him peace, but tonight Garret did not find peace. His heart was too heavy with regret. He was a coward. He should stop his father, but he couldn't, which was what hurt him the most. He inhaled the heady smell of meat roasting on a fire. The men belted bawdy songs overwrought from drink. Garret wished he were back at the castle, away from it all.

His tent flap opened, and Wulf walked in and sat across from him.

"What is going on?" Garret asked his friend. Gone were the days where Wulf held him at bay. He asked him about the change once, and Wulf said he saw something in him worth following.

Wulf picked a handful of peeled chestnuts from a bowl on the table. "Nothing has changed. Your father is still traveling down his path. We will press the advantage and travel at night, laying siege to the castle in two days during the thick of the night like a group of filthy hired hands."

"King Asthmoth won't see us coming, but he won't go down easily," Garret said.

"He won't."

"What can we do?" he asked. There were rules of engagement his father disregarded with his cowardice strategy of attacking during the night without warning.

Wulf exhaled. "Young Prince, there is nothing we can do to help them aside from trying to give them a little warning, but we can't even do that. Your father's witch set some spell around the camp. Nobody can leave without him knowing."

"Alastair," Garret growled. A stream of smoke came from his nose. Both he and his dragon weren't fans of Alistair. "He is the reason for every misfortune that my people have experienced.

Wulf grabbed another handful of chestnuts. "Young prince, we cannot avoid the path in front of us, but remember the blood that he forces us to spill is not on your hands or conscious."

"How is it not Wulf? It will be my sword, so it is my responsibility." Frustrated, Garret pushed his hand in his pocket and reached for his marble. "You're right, we can't avoid it, but we can avenge the lives of the ones that will fall."

Wulf nodded.

"What of the people of Inhous?" he asked.

"The medicine you provided has helped to reduce the spread of disease, but unless we change the conditions of the way they live, we won't be able to contain the disease. It will spread."

His fist hit the table. "I must do more. I can't convince my father to help his people. It's like he's having some sort of standoff with his own people. He dares them to better themselves but gives them no resources. He knows it hasn't rained in years, and the crops have long died, but still, he resists. I have to put an end to this."

"Calm yourself, Young Prince. You have grown much over the years, but you aren't ready to take on your father."

He stood. "If not, now, when? Tell me! How many of my people have to die before I stop being a coward and face my father?"

"Young Prince, you can't allow your emotions to get the best of your logic. If you face your father now and lose, who will provide the small amount of relief that you alone give to those affected by your father's bad decisions? Who will take the throne if you fail? Alastair?"

Garret snarled. "You think me so weak?"

"No, I think your enemy is many, and your allies are few."

Hit by the truth of the matter, Garret's ire calmed. He sat, defeated. "You're right, old dragon. I'm being emotional and throwing a tantrum like a small child. Forgive me."

"There is nothing to forgive, Young Prince." Wulf stood. "Take rest and conserve your strength."

Wulf walked out of the tent without another word, leaving him alone, hating himself and his weaknesses.

TWO DAYS LATER, GARRET was woken by the sun shining through the small holes in the tent's ceiling. He reached up and covered his eyes with his forearm. The sun would dare shine on the eve of a day that would bring death to hundreds, maybe thousands. He could hear the high-pitched chirp of birds as clear as if they perched inside his tent. He laughed dryly. Birds would keep singing oblivious to the surrounding evil, time would keep passing, bringing them closer to the time where death would wash over the land as swift as the sun gave way to darkness at dusk.

He looked at his calloused hands, noting the roughness from years of sword practice. he balled his hands into fists, disgusted with the brutality they would cause tonight. Tonight, the blood of innocent men and women would soak into his skin and stick between his nails, and somehow, he would have to learn how to live with himself afterward.

Garret swung his legs off the makeshift bed in his tent and dressed for the day. Once dressed, he stood, stuffed his hand in his pocket, and gripped his marble, and faced the sun. He slipped on his mask, slowed his gait to slow, lazy, and unconcerned of all matters around him.

Garret heard his name and wanted to pretend he hadn't and continue walking, but he couldn't. This was a show, a game that he had to play for his father's corrupt and easily influenced men.

"There is the prince. He must have some tales to tell as we wait for night to fall."

Garret gripped his marble harder. He didn't want to tell any made up stories of dalliance's that never happened. He didn't want to entertain anyone. What he wanted to do was walk into his father's tent and talk sense into him, and if he failed to do that, then he would run him through with his sword to stop the madness. But he couldn't do that. All he could do was play games with his father and his soldiers—the same soldiers who looked down on him as an incapable prince.

Slowly he turned to face the group of soldiers who called him over with a lazy grin on his face. It was fake. It was all fake, and he was sick of it. He gripped his marble hard before letting it go.

"Well, if it isn't the toothless fairy," Garret said in greeting.

The group of soldiers laughed.

"Ahoy, Prince, that's no way to speak to the man who will stand at your back tonight. Come sit down and tell us a story of one of your conquests with a busty lass."

Garret sat in the middle of the smiling soldiers.

"You will have to be more specific, aren't they all busty lassies?"

The soldiers roared and cheered.

CHAPTER TWELVE

King Athel

King Athel was hours away from reaching his goal of becoming more powerful than any King, human, or dragon before him. He sat among his advisors and listened to them talk about what was to come.

"My King, we should take the forest to the east of the castle, then split into two groups to bring up the rear and push through the front. Our spies have told us King Asthmoth is still unaware of our march. Even if he realizes, he won't be able to gather his soldiers in time to defend himself. We should pack up camp and march forward."

Athel could feel the eager anticipation of an upcoming battle from around the table. They were ready to fight, but he had to be smarter than his base instincts.

"Alastair, what do you think?"

Alastair bowed low, but he knew he wasn't as loyal or subservient as he tried to portray. Alistair had his own agenda, one that he wouldn't let come to pass. His son thought him under Alistair's spell, but his nose worked as well as any dragon's. He could smell the deceit and the witchcraft he tried to work on him. It never worked. He had something stronger than Alastair's petty witchcraft inside of him. He had darkness itself—a creature made from the hate and evil of others. As a dark one himself, hosting a bit of the creature in exchange for the promise of more wealth and power did not cost him at all. Alastair was nothing more than his scapegoat and a very reliable one at that.

"My King, I agree with the commander," Alistair said.

"I see."

He'd already decided to march on the castle this afternoon, but it was always helpful for others to believe they had a hand in his decision. It annoyed him that his son, the one person he wanted to be here, to see how he managed these human idiots, wasn't here. Garret would never become much at the rate he was going on. He hadn't taken part in one pillage as they journeyed through the lands. It was pathetic. "Where is my son?" he asked.

"My King, the last time I saw him, he was telling stories to a few soldiers," Alastair answered.

"I see. Bring him to me immediately."

Athel saw Wulf leave the tent. He assumed it was to retrieve his son. He hated Wulf as much as he hated humans. Wulf and his blessed honor. He saw the way other soldiers watched him in awe. The battles Wulf fought and won for his father were long past. Now, he fought for him, but Athel saw the rebellion lurking deep within his eyes. He paired him with his idiot son to keep him under control. His son did nothing but lie around. He'd hoped Wulf would go stir crazy and maybe jump off a cliff in human form.

His tent flapped opened again, and his son entered. Oddly, his human appearance directly opposed his dragon. His son's dragon was strong and black as the night.

Today, his son pulled his blond hair into a topknot. He looked soft and effeminate. Nothing like Athel, more like his mother. A constant reminder of who he lost. With her beauty, there was little wonder why the human women flocked to the boy, but how could he stomach those human women? There were dragon women he could have, but he hasn't paid them any attention.

Athel narrowed his eyes on his son. "Everyone leave." He waited for the room to clear and watched as the boy sat gracefully on a vacated chair in front of him.

"Why did you not attend the war meeting?"

"I'm sorry, Father, but you know how those meetings bore me to death."

He smirked. "How will you become a king worthy of what I am creating if you don't know how to manage humans and develop war strategy?"

His son looked up at him with a bored expression. Athel couldn't guess if he was putting on an act or if he really was disinterested with the throne. Then his son opened his mouth and confirmed his uselessness.

"Simple, don't die. You must forever rule over the humans and dragons alike. I rather enjoy being the crown prince. I have all the benefits of a king without the duties."

"Worry not dear son. I don't plan on dying anytime soon. It is the death of King Asthmoth that I seek tonight."

"Right, off with his head," He frowned at Garret's smugness.

"Yes, and what will you do during that time?"

His son lifted a brow as if to say was it not obvious what he would do tonight. "Well, Father, I will pillage and kill with the rest of our bloodthirsty soldiers. Mayhap I will find a busty lass and ravish her in my new rooms in the castle. Who knows the night isn't upon us, yet."

Athel let out a groan. "You will fight valiantly beside me, or by the dragon's gods, I will kill you myself. How did I get so lucky to have a son so useless?"

His son stood. "Father, it is better I am useless than ambitious. Count your blessings. Is there anything else?"

"Yes, we leave in two hours, be ready."

"So soon?"

Athel scoffed. "What? Are you scared? What have you learned from all those sword lessons with Wulf?"

"Under Wulf's firm hand, I have gotten rather good at slipping off. I'm not afraid. I just wished I had more time to pack camp and dress in all that heavy sweaty armor."

Athel rolled his eyes. He should have known. The boy was too stupid to be afraid. He'd probably hide behind Wulf. "Go."

CHAPTER THIRTEEN

Aquilla

As Aquilla and Fox walked home, she saw flowers as red as any rose she'd ever seen wrapped in green vines and leaves. It circled what her father said was the oldest tree in the forest. She'd never noticed before.

"Fox, these flowers are new." Aquilla walked toward the tree, amazed that she'd somehow missed such beautiful flowers in all the times she'd walked the path. Aquilla rested her hand on the rough tree bark. Her palm tingled. Power washed over her. She stepped back.

Did that just happen?

Aquilla put her hand back on the tree. The longer she kept it there, the drowsier she became. She sat with her back against the trunk. Her eyes burned with the need to close. She couldn't keep them open. Her thick brown hair curtained the sides of her face as her head fell forward in sleep.

AQUILLA LAY IN A FIELD of beautiful red flowers, the vines wrapped around her like a blanket. She knew she was dreaming. She remembered her eyes' betrayal as she fell asleep against the tree. What she didn't understand was how lucid she dreamed. A cool breeze washed over her, whistling as it passed her.

Aquilla untangled herself and stood. She walked through the field of flowers. As she walked, she saw something in the distance. She walked closer. The closer she came to it the more she could tell it wasn't a something but a someone. A woman stood in front of the tree dressed in a white flowing robe. Her hair and clothing swayed in a breeze Aquilla didn't feel.

The woman's soft, lyrical voice called to her. "Come, child."

Wearily, she took a few steps closer and stopped a few feet outside the woman's reach. "Who are you?" Aquilla asked.

"That's a loaded question, little one."

Aquilla waited until the woman rolled her eyes in defeat.

"I am everything and nothing. I'm the strength, and you are my weakness. Unfortunately, that's the best I can do, right now."

Aquilla pursed her lips. "Is that your name? If so, it's a mouthful."

The woman smiled. Her eyes sparkled with amusement. Her eyes told a story. The woman wasn't human. Human eyes didn't glow. Even so, her ethereal beauty was something to behold. She had a delicate form, which made Aquilla feel inadequate with all of her muscles and round face.

"It is the best I can do. Tell you what. Why don't you give me a name?" One of the woman's perfectly arched brow's lifted in challenge.

Aquilla gave the woman a thoughtful look. She didn't back down from a challenge, not even in her dreams. She wanted a name Aquilla would give her one. Time passed as she thought and dismissed several names including Foxah and Duncaness and moved to colors.

"Lolanthe, after my favorite color."

The woman tilted her head in thought. She whispered the name "Lolanthe," as if she were tasting the flavor of it. "I like it. You can call me Lolanthe. Aside from wanting to know my name, is that the only question you have as you stand in such a sacred place?"

Aquilla smiled. "I'm dreaming, right? It's beautiful and peaceful here, but still a dream, not some sacred place."

Lolanthe smiled. "I agree it is lovely here, but you aren't dreaming. I brought you here through your dreams. There's a slight difference."

Aquilla's brow lifted. "Why?"

"To warn you."

"Warn me of what?" she asked.

Lolanthe's eyes dimmed with regret mixed with pity. She knew that look. Her father looked at her like that whenever he talked about her mother.

"Very soon, there will come a time where you will have to be strong. You need to be stronger than you've ever been before. You will go through many trials, and you will become... different. Embrace your differences because it is your awakening and trust your instincts about people because they will never lead you astray."

Aquilla nodded absently. She had several questions she intended to ask, but before she could, several things happened at once. The ground shook, the once blue sky darkened to gray, and a powerful wind whipped around her, building strength until her hair covered her eyes and strands stuck in her mouth. She lifted her hands and pushed her hair out of her face in time to watch Lolanthe change. Lolanthe's back arched and her body stretched as she watched, mystified. Claws burst out from Lolanthe's feet, her neck stretched, a bright light shone from within, then she disappeared, replaced by a majestic white dragon. Aquilla couldn't breathe. She'd heard tales of dragons. She stepped back slowly, so as not to upset it.

Lolanthe's voice entered her mind. "Do not be afraid of me, Little One. I told you I brought you here to warn you not to harm you. It has begun. Awake Aquilla."

Aquilla woke with a start. Fox growled low with irritation at her side. Darkness had fallen while she slept. Her father would be upset with her, again.

Aquilla frowned down at Fox. "Why didn't you wake me? You know Father will kill me for being out this late."

Fox opened one eye, then the other. He stood and stretched completely unconcerned with her. Aquilla picked up the flower, hoping she could explain what happened to her father if she had proof. She took off running full speed ahead.

SHE RAN AS FAST AS she'd ever run before. Pushed by the need to explain herself to her father. Soon, her instincts took over. A wave of anxiety bubbled in her stomach. Lolanthe's words came back to her. 'Soon you will have to be strong.' And Lolanthe's look of pity haunted her. She had to get home.

When she was a few feet away from home, Fox jumped in front of her growling. He pulled his lips back and showed her his long, sharp teeth.

"What is it? Move, Fox. We have to get home." She tried to run around him, but he cut her off, again. Angry, Aquilla grabbed his neck and moved him aside, then ran around him. She had to get home.

Aquilla ran as fast as she could, careless of her speed and surroundings. Her foot caught on a vine. She fell, hitting the ground hard. Her chin slammed against a sharp rock. Aquilla yelped with pain. She felt the warmth of fresh blood dripping from her open wound, but she didn't stop to take in her condition, because she smelled smoke.

Dense clouds of smoke rose to the skies. Fear weighed her down. Aquilla scrambled off the ground and took off toward the unnatural clouds.

"He put up a good fight. It's a shame we had to put him down. I would have sent him to the Warden at the caves to see him fight Berserker. I bet, he would have won."

Aquilla skidded to a stop at the sound of the male. She hid behind the nearest tree as he and another man dressed in armor walked past her.

Who are they and what are they talking about?

She steeled herself. She had to get closer.

Aquilla pulled her damp hair into a topknot and quietly stepped away, doubling back to appear on the side of the cabin. She was close enough that she could feel the fire's heat on her face. Her cabin wasn't on fire, but some tent made of pieces of wood she'd cut was. Men walked in and out of their cabin. If her father were there, he would have never allowed that. Aquilla's eyes watered. Something awful happened, she knew it. She moved closer but stopped when she saw her father's sword propped against the cabin behind the fire.

Her father's voice filled her mind. "Warriors only part with their swords in death."

Aquilla whispered on the wind, "Only in death."

Rage and grief burned through her blood. She didn't think. She only acted. Aquilla ran, slid, and grabbed her father's sword. Effortlessly, she pulled the sword from the sheath and called to the two soldiers who stood in front of her home.

"Hey, you cowards."

They turned toward her and pulled their swords as they realized she'd leveled hers to strike. After a moment, they attacked. With ease, Aquilla jabbed, defended, attacked, and kicked her opponents. She wasn't fighting well. Her strikes were wild, the same as her rage.

She ran her father's sword across the neck of one soldier. Blood sprayed her face and hair. Still, she didn't hesitate. She kept fighting. The second soldier came for her. She was ready. As Aquilla attacked, grief savaged her mind, but still the men couldn't beat her.

More soldiers joined the fight. She felt minor cuts from swords she couldn't dodge but ignored the pain and pressed on.

"Stand down!"

Aquilla heard the barked command, but she wasn't finished. The men backed down. She tensed to chase the fight, but a man stepped in her path. She snarled at him like Fox snarled at her earlier, showing him her teeth. She'd take him on. She'd take them all.

He drew his sword. Aquilla readied herself. The vibrations of their swords clashing ran up her arms. She gritted her teeth and faced off with the man.

"Who are you?" he bit out.

Aquilla growled, "I am everything and nothing at all."

He hesitated. Aquilla used his hesitation to her advantage and head-butted him. He stumbled back. She lifted her sword, intending to run him through, but he gathered himself. Turning his sword, he pushed the hilt into her stomach. Aquilla doubled over from the un-expected blow. Before she could recover, he punched her in the side of her head.

The last thing she remembered thinking was she held her sword un-til the end.

GARRET STAYED ON HIS horse and watched as Wulf lay the boy who fought like a demon atop his horse. There was something familiar about the way the boy moved, but Garret put it behind him. They didn't have time for any of this.

"What happened here?" Garret asked Wulf.

"Nothing good."

"Was there a family inside? Did they-Did they do something awful to them?" Garret asked.

"Probably, but this boy survived. I won't leave him behind to find the same fate as his family," Wulf said.

"No, we won't do that, but we are marching to a battle. What will you do with him?"

"Sit him somewhere safe and return for him afterward."

CHAPTER FOURTEEN

Lilah

Lilah couldn't sleep. Her mate was asleep next to her oblivious of what was to come if her dream was true at all. There were times over the months she doubted her dream was real. At times she thought of it as a figment of her imagination. She thought it her subconscious dreaming her deepest desires, but still, tonight was the night her mate would pay for what he'd done to their daughter and granddaughter, for what he'd done to her.

Lilah waited for the sign the darkness told her would come at the stroke of midnight. Soon midnight would be upon them, and the truth would tell.

The bell rang twelve times. Now, there should be three crows sitting on her window, and that meant she was to run to the secret tunnel and wait for the morning to arrive then escape. Carefully, she pulled the covers off and slipped her feet into her slippers. Lilah walked to the window on shaky legs. What would she see there? After all this time, she'd hoped to see three crows. As she stood at the window, she saw nothing. Lilah's heart fell with disappointment. As she turned away from the window, she heard the caw of a bird. She whirled around just in time to see one crow perch on her windowsill. Joined by two more, that made three.

Her dream was real, which meant she had to run. Now. Lilah grabbed her cloak and ran to the door, careful not to wake Asthmoth.

Once in the hall, she turned left, then stopped three doors down on the right. She pushed the door open and ran to the back wall where their family crest hung. Lilah pushed it aside and felt for the knob. She pressed hard on the knob and waited for the wall to swing open. Once inside the wall closed behind her. She sat on the dusty floor, praying she wouldn't be found when whatever was to come came.

LILAH HEARD ONE BLOOD-curdling yell after another in the hallways beyond the room mixed with the clang of steel meeting steel. She couldn't help but feel guilty for knowing something was coming and not trying to save at least her closest maidservant. She was like a sister to her, but it was too late now. What was to come was here, and by the sound of it, the monsters killed with pleasure.

"The castle is under siege; find the queen," she heard beyond her walls of protection. Her heart clenched at the loyalty she'd betrayed all to take down her mate. What kind of dragon was she? This was not the normal behavior of a dragon of the light, she knew that, but she couldn't stop herself. She'd been willing to give anything to put an end to Asthmoth, all in the name of vengeance and vindication.

She didn't need to think hard on who'd come to take the castle. She knew it was King Athel. Who else would be so bold? But he wouldn't hold it long, because her granddaughter was the rightful heir to the throne, and she would take it back. Lilah would help her. At the thought of Aquilla and the future they had together, she calmed. Nothing meant more to her than Aquilla.

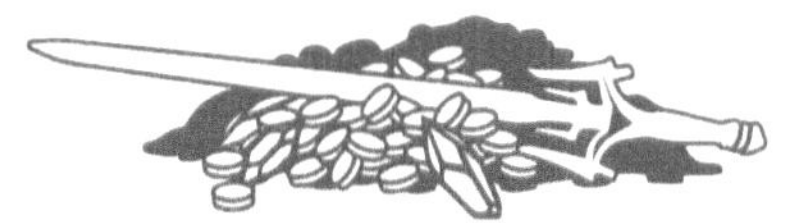

IT WAS MORNING. THE screams stopped hours ago. Lilah should be able to leave the passage. She stood and ran through the narrow tunnel out the hatch that opened to the forest, which was the path she needed to get to Duncan's cabin.

Once outside, she ran off the main road so she wouldn't be spotted. After all, she was the missing queen. King Athel would no doubt want her head on a pike next to her mate's to solidify his rule, but he wouldn't have it. She ran faster, leaping over logs and ducking under low-hanging trees. She saw the cabin up ahead and came to a stop.

Lilah didn't want Aquilla to see her for the first time disheveled and ungraceful. If she did, she'd never be able to convince her granddaughter to brush her hair and dress like a lady. She took several deep breaths, ran her hand down her hair, and pulled her cloak close.

As she neared the cabin, she noticed something was wrong. She smelled smoke, but she saw no fire. *What happened?* Dread pulled her down. Fear made her run. Outside of the cabin, she saw a pyre. She didn't pay it attention. Instead, she banged on the door calling for Duncan and Aquilla. Neither answered. She reached down and turned the knob, shocked to find the door unlocked. Duncan was crazed about locking the doors and windows since Aquilla snuck out some years ago. Something had to have happened.

Lilah pushed the door open and ran inside, calling for Duncan or Aquilla as she ran through the small cabin. Neither Duncan nor Aquilla answered, and neither were anywhere to be found. Inside Aquilla's room, Lilah dropped down to her knees beside her bed and cried. How could everything have gone wrong? Where were they? Gathering her courage, Lilah went back outside. She walked toward the pyre. She pressed her hand against the black logs. The fire had recently died out, from the feel of the wood. She walked around the pyre, looking for any sign or clue as to where Aquilla and Duncan could have gone. Then she noticed what she'd missed in haste to find them in the cabin. She missed the blood that soaked the ground. Duncan's sword was gone.

There wasn't any blood in the house, so whatever happened to them, happened outside. There were depressions in the grass from horses.

Lilah covered her mouth with her hand.

"No, no, this couldn't happen," she said as realization struck her that King Athel's army passed this way on their march to the castle. She knew Duncan would have fought them off to protect Aquilla. He wouldn't let anything happen to her, and she was trained as well. Aquilla had to be alive. She had to be, and if she were alive, she'd come home, so Lilah would wait for her granddaughter to return. She knew Aquilla was alive. She could feel it.

CHAPTER FIFTEEN

Garret

Garret walked through the halls of King Asthmoth's—no, that's wrong, his father's new castle. His father tasked him to look for any survivors. He didn't specify what he should do when he found them, but Garret could figure it out.

He didn't find anyone he thought he couldn't keep alive. What good would killing a few maids do for his father? The castle was his. His underhanded siege was successful. Garret returned to his father to report that he hadn't found any survivors. When he heard his father shouting before he saw the man himself.

"How did you lose her?" King Athel boomed.

"We never found her; she wasn't in the castle. We searched everywhere."

Garret wished he could have warned Sorge that failure wasn't an option for his father. It would have been better if he just deserted.

"My King, she isn't here, I promise you this. I can search the city for her."

"No need. Why would I give you the same job twice?" King Athel lifted his sword and ran it across Sorge's throat. Garret didn't speak, he didn't react, he didn't move.

"They are all idiots," his father said before turning toward him.

"What happened, Father?"

"He couldn't find Lilah. Pitiful beast."

Yes, that would set him off.

"It doesn't matter. I have taken the castle. Nothing else matters. She won't hide for long and then I will pay her what she's owed." King Athel walked over the dead man at his feet. Garret heard his father's shoes splashing in the blood he'd spilled without a thought to the life he took. Sorge was a good man with a new wife and son. Garret shook his head. He wouldn't let them suffer because of his father. He'd have to remember to tell Wulf to send coins and supplies to Sorge's family.

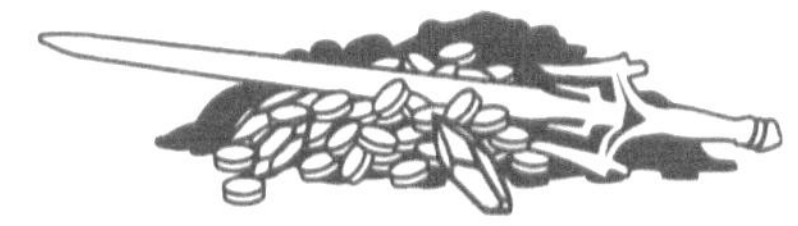

GARRET WALKED AT HIS father's side. They walked outside without speaking, heading to the battlement. He knew, if he looked at his father, he'd see him smiling down at the carnage, so he didn't look at him. He didn't need another reason to want to rid the world of King Athel's destruction; he had enough already.

"Boy, I have accomplished something no other before me has. I have carved my name into the immortal legacy of the archives as the one who accomplished what no other could. This land was ours before the dragons of the light took it from us so many years ago. Now, it is ours again. I've grown my lands far beyond my vision. Look about boy, this is my empire, and I am its emperor. I always knew that I was meant for more. Now is the time for Emperor Athel to reign. Those under my rule will obey."

CHAPTER SIXTEEN

Aquilla

When Aquilla woke, the sun was up, and her head throbbed. Gently, she reached up to the side where she hurt the most. She felt a bump on. She tried to remember where she received it and where she was.

Aquilla closed her eyes as she heard someone approaching.

"I see him, I see him, this be a free slave! I wish they all be so easy to come across."

A man answered. "Stop carrying on. Sun be swiftly fading. Put the boy in the cart and let's be off."

"The boy is sleepin," the man closest to her said.

"Oy, slap him around a bit. Don't be useless, or I'll leave ye for the vultures and take the boy, ye hear."

I'm not a boy. Aquilla slowly opened her eyes.

"Oy, look there, he's awake. Up with you, boy, we have places to go."

Aquilla felt a rough hand wrap around her arm and pull her up.

"There ye go. Come easy. Ye won't like the hard way."

Dazed, Aquilla did as she was told. She wanted to run, but she didn't know where she would go. Her mind was blank. *There was nothing.*

"Stop here, boy."

Again, Aquilla did as she was told, too stunned in the realization that she couldn't remember anything. She heard the clink before she felt the heavy shackles fall, hitting the tops of her feet.

"There ye go, lad. Ye have new jewelry to show off to the others, cept, they have it too!" He laughed. The scar that bisected his top lip stretched. He was a wretched looking creature. She was pushed on to a wagon with thirteen others. The wagon moved, and everyone lurched forward.

THEY'D TRAVEL FAR INTO the night before they stopped. Hope blossomed that maybe she would see something familiar. As quick as her hope rose, it fell. She didn't recognize anything.

The men opened the small door that barely held them all in and pulled them out of the wagon. Aquilla and the others lined up outside a barn. Once they were all out of the wagon, the barn door opened where the two men waited and pushed them inside. The men tripped over each other and received a hard kick to their stomach for their effort.

Each man picked an unlit torch from outside the barn door and lit them. At least now she could see the ground.

Once inside the barn, she noticed the silhouette of more people sitting grouped in a corner in silence.

They are all men.

"Oy, ye heathens be sleepin here for the night. Don't be trying to escape. We will hunt ye down, and ye won't like what happens. Ye the Emperor's property now!" he laughed. His laughter ended in a coughing fit. Aquilla hoped he choked.

She moved closer to the wall behind her. The silence was unbearable. By not speaking, she felt like that meant she gave up, and she didn't want to give up. She wanted to escape.

"Hey, I'm Fox."

Aquilla jumped and let out a stifled cry.

"Sorry, I just wanted to introduce myself."

"I'm Aquil—" she stopped herself. Aquilla couldn't use her proper name. She needed a boy's name, but again, her mind blanked. Anxiety crept along the edges of her mind.

What's wrong with me?

"Did you say your name was Aquillo?"

Aquilla grabbed for the name. "Yes, yes, Aquillo. That's my name."

"Nice to meet you. Who blessed you with the gift of slavery? For me, a wench promised me a night of passion I'd never forget. She was right about one thing. I'll never forget how she took my coins and clothes, then left me for the slavers. When I escape this place, I won't ever be that stupid again, and I'll repay her kindness."

"Why didn't you fight back?" Aquilla whispered, her interest piqued by the scandal.

"Against the wench? She drugged me. Usually, I'd never fall for such a vile trick, but I had my reasons."

Aquilla hid a smile. "The night of passion?" she teased.

He grunted.

"So what about you? How did you end up here?"

Aquilla shrugged playing down her worry over her missing memories. "I don't know. I can't remember anything before waking up against a tree except for my name. After I woke, these men pulled me into a wagon and shackled me."

"You can't remember anything?"

"No. Nothing. When I try to remember, it hurts a little. Honestly, the only thing I remember is my name. There are echoes of memories, like words without faces, thoughts without understanding of how or why I know to have them. Whenever I try to focus on something, I lose the thought and my mind slips back into a blank state."

"That's too bad. Something must have hit you hard on the head to knock the sense and memories out of you. How about we look after each other, like brothers?"

"I don't want to be your brother."

"You say that now, but I have a charming personality, plus it will be easier to survive if we watch out for each other. I've heard the dreadful stories about the caves."

"Caves? Is that where we are going? Why?" Aquilla asked.

"You don't know?"

"I wouldn't have asked if I did," Aquilla said in what she hoped was a male voice.

"The conqueror of our fine land is building a city within a cave. Stupid if you ask me, but every month the Emperor sends a fresh batch of men to work the caves. Some men are serving sentences, and some they stole."

"Like you were?"

Fox nodded. "Like me and you."

"Are there any women there?"

"No. I'd think babies would be an issue if they mixed the men with women."

Despair washed over Aquilla. How much longer could she pass for a male?

"So Aquillo, back to it, will you be my brother?"

Aquilla couldn't see a reason not to be. "Yes, we can be brothers."

"I have a good feeling about this," Fox said.

Aquilla smiled. Fox pushed himself closer to her and fell asleep with his head on her shoulder. She wanted to push him off, but there was something about his weight against her that felt familiar. Aquilla let him stay. As he drifted off to sleep, she heard him mumble.

"So glad we are together again."

But she'd just met Fox, hadn't she?

CHAPTER SEVENTEEN

Garret

Garret walked around the castle, searching for a place he could carve out as his. The only prerequisite he had was the location. His room had to be far, far away from his father's rooms.

He opened the door to his left and covered his nose. The smell of old blood permeated the place. They would need to do something about that soon before it bled into the wood. He backed out and closed the door. Garret kept walking a few feet before finding another door to his left. He opened it and smiled. No smells, only dust, which he could handle. He walked into the room and pulled off his boots, sword, and shirt before he fell on the bed and drifted to sleep.

THE SOUND OF SLAMMING doors woke Garret in what he hoped was the morning. He groaned his protest and rolled onto his back, debating his next steps. He could find someone to help prepare a bath, he could find out who was approaching, or he could lay there uncaring. He stayed put.

The door to his temporary lodging swung open.

"Prince Garret?"

Garret smiled when he realized who called him. He would always recognize this old dragon. She wore a simple gray dress with her graying hair pulled into a tight bun. He loved how she embraced the humans; she even spoke like them. She didn't have to clean and take care of him and his father. But as long as he could remember, Gertrude had always been at his side, sneaking in and out of his rooms to clean and fret over him.

"Gertrude, how are you today? Did you have to travel through the night to get here?"

"Ay, me Prince, the soldiers woke me up in the dead of night. They jostled me and handled me roughly. They yelled about the Kin—I mean Emperor wanting me here before he woke this morn. I'll not thank him for that."

"Of course not. You need your beauty sleep," Garret teased.

"You be joking on me. My face is no grand beauty. I'll leave you to your peace, my Prince. There's much work to be doing here."

"Thank you."

She nodded and left. Garret sighed. He wouldn't be able to go back to sleep.

GARRET WALKED THROUGH the hallways bustling with servants pushing mops across the floors and switching out the water when it turned red.

Garret tried to ignore the pain in his heart at the thought of what he did the night before. He was the reason the water turned red. He left the servants behind and turned down a corridor filled with arching windows. He looked out of the windows and watched as men carried body after body off the landscape. The truth wounded him. All of what happened was because he wasn't strong enough to stop his father.

Garret balled his hands into fists and made a promise he would die to keep.

"I will become stronger. I will take him down."

CHAPTER EIGHTEEN

Aquilla

"Wake up, you lazy peasants."

Aquilla woke. For a split second, she didn't remember where she was, then the memories of the day before rushed to the surface. Fox still slept at her side. She nudged him.

"Hey, Fox. We better get up."

He growled at her. Reflexively, she slapped his nose. Shocked at herself, she pulled her hand back.

"I'm sorry," she said hurriedly.

He stretched. "Must you always do that?" he asked.

"Do what?"

Fox shook his head. "No, I said, I always do that."

"Do what?" she repeated.

"Growl when I'm forced to wake up early."

He gave her a sheepish smile before standing. Aquilla stood next to him. She was filthy. She smelled awful. Dirt stuck in her nails, and her hands felt sticky from the sweat and grime she gained during her travels.

"I'll stay behind you so we can stay together," Fox said.

Aquilla nodded. She looked around. Men were lining up against the far wall of the barn. She wondered what stopped them from overpowering their two captors to steal back their freedom. They'd captured over twenty men. They could do it if they worked together.

Someone needed to lead the charge, start the fight, rebel against the injustice of being stolen against one's will.

Thoughts whirled in her mind. The need to take action was building inside her.

Rebel, rebel, echoed in her mind and churned, gathering momentum, adding more words to her internal storm: attack, fight, freedom. Her body vibrated with anticipation. She had to say the words. She had to get away; they all did. Her mouth opened to scream her frustration and push these men to act, but a hand on her shoulder stopped her. Her eyes traveled up, starting at the dirty hand, and ending with her staring into Fox's familiar eyes. He shook his head and mouthed, "Not now."

Aquilla wanted to shake his hand off and proceed, but she didn't. She stayed in line, quiet with her head down.

AFTER HOURS OF SITTING under the sun as they traveled to their destination, Aquilla was hot, sweaty, and thirsty. She looked around the wagon, glancing at the men around her. A few were slumped with their eyes closed. She didn't know if they'd fainted or were sleeping, but she knew they were alive by the rise and fall of their chests. She spied an older man hunched in the wagon's corner, nestled between the door and the bench. Sweat drenched his shirt. His face was red from the sun burning his skin. He may not last the journey. The wagon came to a stop. One man walked toward the back and released the door.

"Oy, you filthy beasts. Ye step out of the cart and drink from the pond with the horses. Ye may want to watch for the gator. Last week it leaped up and swallowed a man whole. Me seen it with me own eyes, but ye have only two choices. Drink from the gator water or do not drink a'tall."

Fox leaned over and mumbled, "I should throw him into the gator water."

Aquilla grunted in agreement.

"Oy, pretty boy, ye have words for me?"

Aquilla's body stiffened. Fox shook his head in answer. But that wasn't enough for the vile man.

"Nay, methinks ye do."

Fox shook his head again. The man took a few steps toward Fox, but Aquilla stepped in his path. She couldn't explain why she stood between them, but she did, and it felt right. Her body tensed, and her blood rushed, readying to fight. If this awful man wanted to pick on someone, he could pick on her, not her friend.

Aquilla stared at the man. Her eyes shone with determination. Her body vibrated with anticipation. *Come on and give me a reason.*

After an intense moment, her captor backed down. Fox pulled her toward the pond.

"Thank you for your show of bravado, but I could have handled him," he said.

She looked at Fox with one eye lifted in disbelief.

"I could have," Fox protested.

She smiled. "Sure, you could."

"I'm not joking. I have a list of men I've bested in my life. Some names on the list would surprise you."

"I'm sure they would," she teased. "Come on, let's drink some water, you first," she said, laughing out loud at Fox's shocked expression.

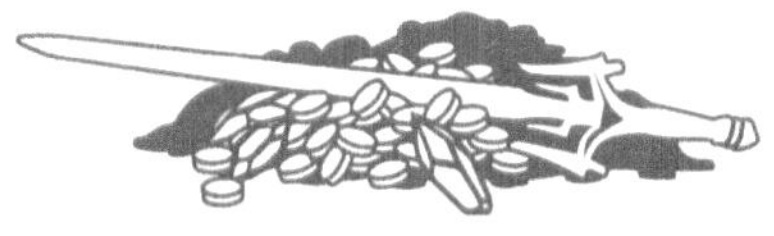

AFTER SPENDING SCANT time at the pond, they traveled until the sun lingered in the sky, waiting for her dark lover.

Aquilla caught the memory of a story told to her long ago. The face of the storyteller escaped her mind and so did the place, but she heard the words as if she were living the memory over as a spectator instead of a participant. He started the way all storytellers start tragic tales.

In the beginning, there were many types and colors of dragons. Some were big some were small, but there were only two sects, the dark, and the light. The dark ones craved power and wealth. Nothing was off the table. If having wealth meant holding the most land, then they wanted it all. If having wealth meant having jewels, then they would have them all and they believed dragons should rule overall. Then there were the dragons of light, who wished to coexist with all creatures and benefit the whole instead of the one. They understood harmony in all things. They stopped the dark from using their greed to destroy the land by taking all the resources. The light was the ying to the dark's yang. Together they brought balance, stopping each other from going too far one way or the other, but they never mixed.

Until Prince Damascus of the Dark realized the one possession he'd never had and wanted more than any gold or land was Princess Priscilla of the light's love, so he pursued her with the same intensity he would any other treasure. At first, she wouldn't give him the time of day, but Damascus didn't relent. He kept taking risks to see her, and each time he brought her a beautiful treasure and promise of eternal devotion. Soon, Priscilla fell in love with Damascus. She embraced him as he was, and he embraced her. They both changed little by little as their forbidden romance blossomed in their hearts. Priscilla became more aggressive in a fight. She wanted to be the best and the strongest dragon that ever existed; she trained with Damascus. He taught her everything he knew, and she absorbed it all. Likewise, she taught Damascus about balance and how even darkness needed balance to survive. Damascus stopped striving to have it all. Now he wanted to have enough. Underhanded means like trickery and thievery were still on the table, but not underhanded means that hurt the whole. He wouldn't scorch the ground, because it destroyed the crops, he wouldn't eat all the cows because then there wouldn't be more. He understood the difference. He'd eat enough. He would have enough.

But soon, dragons noticed the changes in them both, and rumors circulated. Damascus and Priscilla knew they shouldn't meet, but they couldn't help it. They loved each other greatly. Then one day, they were followed. They wouldn't know it until days later when their enemies captured them. They demanded the Prince and Princess to stop seeing each other and arranged marriages for them with proper dragons of each sect. Priscilla and Damascus refused. They only wanted each other. The other dragons were upset, and cries of treason rang from both factions. Refusing to deny their love for each other left the two kings with no other choice but to put the two lovers to death for treason. Even then, Priscilla and Damascus wouldn't deny their love. Their desperation and conviction reached the gods who took notice and pity upon the two dragons and approved of their love. It was too late for them to save Priscilla and Damascus by the time they realized what was happening, so they saved their spirits. Priscilla and Damascus's spirits flew up beyond the sky.

The world shook, and everything changed. The gods roared their disapproval at both kings for their cruelty.

"Every day, in the skies, you will see the two lovers and be reminded of their unconditional love. Priscilla of the light will bring light to the world every day, and Damascus of the dark will bring darkness to this world every night. No longer will you enjoy the fruits of our kindness. The predators that thrive in darkness will stalk you as you stalked Priscilla and Damascus. And for your insolence, every day at dusk, you will watch Priscilla and Damascus embrace. Nowhere in this world can you avoid and dismiss their eternal love. And as for Priscilla and Damascus, one day, we will allow their spirits to return to this world to reunite. When they reunite, we will gift them the world to rule and the power to defeat the evil you all gladly accepted in your hearts to fuel your cruelty."

Aquilla wished the gods would notice her now. What she and all the people around her were going through was injustice, but there weren't any gods listening to her cries. No, they were laughing at her while they sat back and enjoyed her torment. They took her memories, forced her to disguise herself as a boy, taunted her by allowing her to remember one thing from her past... a story about the love she'd never have and gods that cared but not about her.

CHAPTER NINETEEN

Garret

On another day, Garret wouldn't react to watching the witch huddled in whispers with his father, but today, his guilt and frustrations ate away at him, and the sight of both his father and the witch upset him. He stood with Wulf in the center of his father's newly aquired study and waited for his father to acknowledge his presence. Impatient, Garret cleared his throat. His father looked up, shocked to see he stood in front of him. He wouldn't be there had his father not called him.

"Sit down," his father said. Garret gripped his marble and thought sourly that the show he made of himself must go on. He forced what he hoped appeared as a genuine smile and carefree attitude.

"Father, you look well. It seems everything is coming together for you." He sat down on a chair in front of his father, who sat at what used to be King Asthmoth's desk. A disarray of papers was spread over the surface, as if he were looking for something. Garret filed that bit of information for later.

"Of course, I am the emperor, and I have amassed more wealth than any king before me. What's there to be unwell about?"

Garret let his brow rise. "Nothing at all, Father. It's just a saying."

His father narrowed his eyes. "Keep your sayings to yourself. I called you here because King Daemon and his daughter Princess Esmeralda will arrive in six weeks. I need this place ready for their arrival. I want the arena finished, and Alistair will tend the structural issues with the castle. If King Daemon treaties with us, we will have more land and power. I need you on your best behavior with Princess Esmeralda."

"Are you planning a tournament, Father? Is that why you need the arena finished?" Garret asked as an idea formed.

"Yes, of course, nothing says power better than having the best in the land fight for you, don't you think?"

Garret nodded his agreement.

"Yes, this will be a grand event. As long as you can get the arena finished in time, which I'm sure you will."

"I will, because you asked it of me, but isn't having a tournament like all the other tournaments plain? If you really want to show King Daemon only the best come to you, why don't you invite the best swordsmen of the land to compete against each other in several games? The last man standing would be the winner and named something like the Emperor's Sword."

His father's brow raised. "I like where you're going. I should only have the best. What better way to prove I have everything anyone could desire? I must have this person. Everyone will want him, but only I will have him. I like it. I like it all! Marvelous, Garret, and I like the name Emperor's Sword. Of course his name should include the name of his owner. Alistair!" the Emperor yelled.

"Yes, emperor," Alistair said and bowed deeply. Garret tried not to show his disgust.

"Commission a sword worthy of the best swordsmen in the land. I will present it to the man and confer the title myself."

Garret's mind fired with ideas. He could find the best swordsman, train him to win, then when his father presented him with the sword, he would strike his father down for good. It was a loose plan, but one that was achievable with the right person holding the sword, and he would find the right person.

"That sounds like a splendid idea, Father. I will begin my work."

WULF AND GARRET WALKED out of his father's study.

"I know what you're thinking, Wulf, and I had a good reason to lead my father this way."

"You don't know what I'm going to say. I need not know your thoughts to trust you, and I do trust you. I trust you to do the right things for the kingdom, so whatever you are planning, I will help you."

Garret smiled. "Thank you, Wulf, that means a lot to me."

CHAPTER TWENTY

Aquilla

When they reached the caves, it was well after dark. The biting bugs had begun their descent, attracted to her rotten smell. Her legs itched to the point of distraction, but she didn't scratch. Now that they were stopped at a cave entrance, she forgot her bites and focused on what was to come.

A round man with a bald head and one eye that traveled the opposite direction of the other appeared at the gate. She'd never seen this man before. "Oy, it is time ye freeloaders make some coin to pay for the ride here. We don't be paying for transporting people for free, ye know. That'll not be good business."

He opened the gate, and the older man who sat slouched sweating in the corner fell face forward on to the ground. The round men bent over, then kicked the old man's feeble body.

"Unhook em from the other one. The moon is only getting higher, and me eyes are getting heavier. Need to get this lot cliffside, then make it to me bed. I been waiting on yer arrival for a time."

"Not our fault. We—"

The round man lifted a hand. "It never be yer fault, but I know it really is. Stop yer babbling like a mother. I'll not be put on by ye. Come on, ye bunch of ugly backsides of a gremlin. Get in the cave."

They followed the round man into the cave.

THE PATH THEY WALKED held just enough light to see the outline of the person in front of her but not enough to know who it was. The air smelled damp and musty as they traveled farther into the cave. Before long, Aquilla could hear the clanking sound of metal hitting stone. Judging from the sounds coming from somewhere deeper in the cave, there were already a number of men here working on this project of the Emperor's. Aquilla frowned and her brows creased. How many people had they taken? Her heart ached at the thought of families searching for their fathers or brothers only to lose hope of ever finding them.

Is someone searching for me? She tripped over a rock and fell hard to her knees. She gritted her teeth against the pain.

"Are you okay?" Fox asked pulling her up off the ground.

"Fine, thank you."

"No problem, get moving, we don't want to be beaten so soon after arriving."

Aquilla nodded and sped up her pace, catching up with the tall man in front of her.

They turned left into another tunnel, and the sounds were louder, and the smell changed. The musty smell was gone replaced by the sharp tang of explosives and sweat.

The tunnel opened into another part of the cave. Aquilla couldn't see much. Even here the light was too dim to make out the details, but she could see that they were building something inside the cave. There had to be another twenty or thirty men here working on the framework of a building.

What had Fox said? 'A city within a cave'. If that were the case, they had a lot of work to do.

"Ye see where ye be working from this day to the end of ye miserable lives? But not tonight. Yer master be kind and gives ye the night off. Follow me. I'll show ye to your deluxe bed chambers."

Aquilla heard someone to her left chuckle. She turned her head, squinting through the dim lighting to see who it could have been. There were several guards standing there. She couldn't tell if there were more. She filed the information away.

The group moved through the cave toward another tunnel. Once they passed through the tunnel, they reached another open area.

"Ye would want to watch yer steps here. This be a cliff's edge and where ye sleep."

How could they see the edge? It was darker here than it was in any other part of the cave she'd been in. More guards followed them in. After a short while, she realized what they were doing. They were removing their shackles. She'd suppose those weren't needed any longer.

"Find an empty straw cot and ye can have it. Enjoy yer stay. Ye will meet the warden tomorrow at yer morning meal."

Aquilla and Fox found two straw cots next to each other and claimed those. Aquilla could smell the stench of used straw. It smelled like old urine and body order.

"I can't sleep on this," she told Fox.

He hummed his agreement. "This is certainly not a deluxe bed chamber as he promised."

Aquilla rolled her eyes. "Of course not."

"Move aside. Let me help. Who knows what is crawling within the straw." Fox gagged as he bent over the straw cot.

"What are you doing?"

"Magic. Now, shut up."

Aquilla was going to protest but the smell that wafted from her cot did improve. She moved closer to Fox. The smell was completely gone.

How did he do that?

Aquilla opened her mouth to ask but was cut off by Fox.

"Do not ask me how I did that because I already told you. Now, excuse me, I need to take care of my straw cot. Honestly, the things I put up with for you," he mumbled to himself.

CHAPTER TWENTY-ONE

Aquilla

Aquilla woke with a kick to her kidneys.

"Wake up. This place won't build itself. Wake up, ye freeloading scum."

Aquila opened her eyes still somewhat dazed and confused, but her mind quickly caught up with the situation. She turned toward Fox's cot.

"Fox, are you awake?"

"How could I not be with that man yelling at the top of his lungs and kicking me in the back?"

"He kicked me in my kidneys. If that makes you feel better."

"It doesn't, thank you."

Aquilla stood and felt an immediate urgency to relieve herself. Fear wrapped around her. How could she relieve herself? She couldn't go around the other men or she'd be exposed. With her luck, once they found out she wasn't a man, they'd probably kill her.

Aquilla bit her lip. The more she thought about her need for relief, the more she had to go. She pinned her legs together. She needed a solution.

"Why are you standing like that?" Fox asked.

"I have to, um, relieve myself in the worst way."

Fox lifted a hand. "I'm sure you can pee over there," Fox pointed to the gaping chasm in front of them "you won't hit someone on the head.

Go on. I'll wait over here, then take my turn. You seem a little squeamish around other men."

Aquilla shook her head.

Blasted. "I'll be back. Don't wait for me if the group moves. I'll catch up."

"Where are you going, Aquillo?" Fox asked.

"To pee!" she yelled. then jogged in the opposite direction of the group, frightfully aware of the edge of the cliff as she ran. Finally, she reached an isolated area. She looked left and right. There were no cots and no other men. With her back against the cave wall, she pushed her pants down and relieved herself. Her bladder clenched with thanks.

Aquilla caught up with the group. They walked through a tunnel that led back to the area where they would work. Just before the right turn up ahead, the group turned left into another tunnel.

Really, how big is this cave?

This tunnel opened into another area where there were benches and tables made of the stone from the cave. The other men sat. Aquilla lifted a brow to Fox before realizing it was too dark to see her face. Fox sat down first, then Aquilla joined him. A bowl of something terrible sat in front of them.

Aquilla quietly leaned over and asked Fox. "What is this?"

"Looks like the mix I've seen people feed to pigs."

"I can't eat this," she said, her stomach both growling in hunger and turning in disgust.

"I know, but we need to eat. We need fuel. Close your eyes and hold your breath while you eat it."

"Why would I do that?" she asked.

"So, you can't taste it."

Aquilla did as she was told, but she still tasted the pig mix and the thick lard like substance stuck to the top of her mouth. She gagged.

"You better not throw up on me or near me. That is disgusting."

She gagged again.

"I mean it Aquillo, take this like a man."

"I can't. It's... oh my god," Aquilla said, her gagging worsening.

"Aquillo, stop it. You are embarrassing me in front of the other men."

Aquilla told herself to stop gagging. She just needed to swallow it. She could do that. The other men were beginning to stare.

There was a commotion at the tunnel entrance rapturing the men's interest from her to the entrance. Several guards came in, followed by the silhouette of a round man. He stopped in front of the group. His belly hung far over the waist of his pants.

"Listen. Listen. Heathens. I am the warden over this pit of hell. You live because of my kindness. I keep you fed. I keep straw on your lice infected cots. Most of you know this already, but some of you lot are recent additions. Let me be clear. Nobody disobeys my rules of which I only have one; do whatever I say. If anyone disobeys, the pit of fire awaits. There is no short supply of you heathens, so if I lose a few nobody will care. None of you will leave this place alive, so whether I kill you or you kill yourself matters not to me, so don't go trying to threaten me with your life. I couldn't care less. Your job is to make sure we stay on track of turning this hell hole into an underground city."

He laughed at this. "Personally, I think the Emperor just wants to kill you sorry lot. We've been working for years, and we have progressed a little. It's slow going, you know, because it is a blasted cave and all. Nevertheless, use your pick to hit things and make some sort of progress, just enough to keep the Emperor pleased."

After he finished, he turned and left with his men.

"LET'S GO HIT THINGS over there." Fox pointed to a group of men huddled together, working on a piece of the cave wall.

Aquilla nodded. "Looks good."

They walked over with their picks in hand. The men were working silently. The only thing they had in common between them was the proximity. Fox looked at her then at the men and shrugged. He walked straight to the wall and began pounding at the cave wall.

"What are you doing?" Aquilla asked loud enough to be heard over the sound of the picks clanging against the stone.

"I don't know. I'm just going to hit here and then there and see what happens."

Aquilla couldn't argue. They weren't given any instruction. She began hitting the stone. Each time her pick struck the unmovable stone, vibrations ran up her arm. After a while, she switched arms and kept trying to make a deeper mark where she hit. It was when she changed the pick to her right hand and wiped the sweat from her forehead that she realized how hot she was. "Are you hot?" she asked Fox.

"My shirt is clinging to my back with sweat. It's a bit disgusting."

Aquilla looked around at the other men. One man fell, landing with a loud thud on his backside. The noise alerted the guard, who didn't hesitate to pull out a whip and bring it down hard on the man's back.

"Get up! Or I swear I will beat you until your last breath."

Aquilla tensed.

"Stop staring, Aquillo. How would you like it if someone stared at you while you were punished?"

"This isn't right. The man did nothing wrong. He's just exhausted." Aquilla took a step toward the guard with his whip poised to come down against the older man again. Fox pulled her sleeve.

"What are you doing?" he whispered.

"That man did nothing wrong. I need to help him."

"No, Aquillo, stay put and mind your business. Do you see anyone else jumping to the man's aid? No, learn to take cues from those around you."

A flash of pain scorched the skin on Aquilla's back. The sensation shocked her. She dropped her pick before turning to face a smiling guard.

"Why are ye talking when ye should be working?" the guard asked.

The guard raised his arm, intending to slam the whip down again. Aquilla reached out, caught the whip, and pulled. When the guard was close enough, she slammed her fist into the guard's face.

He stumbled before righting himself. The guard put his fist up to fight her, and she did the same. Instinct took over as she sunk into position. The guard shouted threats and curses at her, she ignored them all and focused on her goal. *Concentrate on the fight.*

"I will teach you, boy, who is in charge around here," was the last thing he said before Aquilla attacked. She lunged for him—her fist connected with his stomach. The guard bent over in pain, then Aquilla rammed her fist up and connected right under the guard's chin, snapping his head back. The guard fell to the ground, unmoving, but she knew he was alive because his chest moved up and down. A small part of her wanted to stop. A larger part of her wanted to finish him. She wanted him to pay for all the misdeeds he no doubt caused those around her and those before her. Then, an echo of a memory stopped her. The memory of a familiar yet faceless voice, deep and full of authority, said one word, which was enough.

"Honor."

Aquilla pulled back and stood over the guard, her breaths came fast as some insignificant echo of a memory that demanded her to remain honorable held her back, but only barely.

Then, she realized her mistakes. She only made two. One, fighting the guard in the first place, and two, not paying attention to all the guards that moved on her. It was her misfortune that she realized these two things after she felt the terrible pain of another whip slam down on her back, then another one in quick succession until she turned around arms up to protect her face only for the guards to continue whipping her with strike after strike until blood dripped from her arms and stomach. Her last thought as the final blow landed on the top of her head was that she should have listened to Fox.

CHAPTER TWENTY-TWO

Garret

Garret stood inside the arena, impressed by the progress, and distressed at how their people worked from dusk until dawn. As he walked around the arena, he engaged the workers as best he could.

"How's the little one?" he asked one worker who shared with him that his wife recently delivered their first child.

"Very good. She is growing bigger every day." Garret smiled at him and walked on.

Garret yelled up to a worker who was one of the men who held the laborious task of laying the bricks. "Carey, be careful up there, my good man. We can't afford to lose you!" The man smiled a toothless smile and saluted.

Garret heard Gregorio before he saw his small, slender figure. "You will work if you don't want the Emperor to chop off your head. Make no mistake. I will serve it up to him personally to avoid a similar fate."

Garret shook his head. "Gregorio, I don't think anyone will lose their heads today."

Gregorio turned to face him. His light brown tunic and brown pants hung from his thin body. Garret knew as long as there was one person still working, Gregorio would be there next to him. For all the bravado and harsh words, he was a fair manager.

"My Prince, what brings you here?"

"Just checking in. Unlike you all, my neck really is on the line."

Gregorio shook his head in disagreement. "Your father would never harm his heir."

Garret lifted a brow, questioning Gregorio's assumptions. "Are you sure?"

Gregorio's face paled. He turned around and walked toward his workers. "Get back to work. All of you, get back to work," he clapped his gnarled hands together. "I mean it. Anyone caught dallying will be whipped!" Gregorio looked back at Garret again, then added, "maybe even to death."

Garret held back his grin. Gregorio never whipped a worker unless they did something unconscionable. He doubted anyone took the threat seriously.

"Gregorio, don't be so bloodthirsty. I will leave you to your work and come again another day."

Gregorio waved him away. Garret walked back to his rooms in the east wing of the castle.

CHAPTER TWENTY-THREE

Aquilla

When Aquilla woke, everything around her was pitch black, a true darkness devoid of any light. She couldn't see her hand as she lifted it to her eyes. She couldn't see anything at all. She felt the heat of the ground hot against her skin. The longer she lay on the hot ground, the more she became aware of the pain. Aquilla felt several open and bleeding wounds on her body. She had many small ones. She shrank in fear. Voices filled her mind.

I thought you were strong.

I taught you better than this.

Are you a quitter? A worthless girl?

"I'm not weak," she whispered to the voices.

Then why aren't you fighting?

Indeed. Why wasn't she? She was strong, and there was nothing that could weaken her more than fear. She pulled her courage and packed her fear away. She could get up, and she would save herself and those she'd promised. But even courage couldn't fight her body's need to slow itself. Her eyes grew heavy as the searing pain against her back pulled her unconscious again.

AQUILLA'S EYES OPENED, and she braced herself for the pain, but it never came. Aquilla didn't move. She didn't open her eyes, afraid that if she did, she'd have an onslaught of pain, and she'd already made her mind up to escape the pit of darkness, so she couldn't keep passing out.

Slowly, Aquilla peeled herself off the ground and moved into a crawling position. It wasn't until her hands lay flat against the stone that she noticed it wasn't hot anymore. She stood with no pain. Aquila flexed her muscles. She was perfectly fine. She saw light ahead. Where was she and how did she get here? She knew she was deeper in the cave before. Aquilla pressed a hand against the cave wall to steady herself against a wave of dizziness. She felt marks on the wall. She moved her hand over them. They were deep claw marks.

What lives inside this cave that can cause such large deep claw marks?

Whatever it was, she didn't want to stick around to meet it. She walked forward toward the light. Once she entered the cave opening, several guards turned and stared at her for a while before remembering to pull out their swords. Aquilla lifted her arms in surrender.

"I come in peace," she said.

Several more guards came, and they all surrounded her. She left her hands up while the guards talked and gesticulated wildly, trying to decide what to do with her. More than once, she heard that she should be dead. *That is nice of them.* Finally, a decision had been made, and they pushed her forward. She walked with them freely because she was unwilling to see the pit again anytime soon.

AQUILLA AND THE GUARDS walked through several tunnels until she was ordered to wait outside in a well-lit area, which annoyed her as it was obvious, they purposefully kept the rest of the cave barely visible.

The warden appeared in front of her. Aquilla thought it would be better if she couldn't see him. He was balding, but he combed the few remaining strands over the bald spot. It didn't help hide the fact that he was bald. It only drew more attention to it. He was bigger than she'd thought. He had multiple chins that moved whenever he did. Not to mention the loud colors he wore. There wasn't a pattern, just several bold colors patched together.

"Is this him?" the warden asked.

A guard pushed her forward. "Yes, this is him. He just walked out. Unscathed. It's madness."

"Impossible!" the warden said.

"Sir, it is true. I assure you. Many of us saw it."

"Come closer, Boy."

Aquilla was shoved forward. She nearly tripped over her own feet. She swallowed the need to push back.

"You, Boy walked out of the pit alive?"

"I did," she said, and stood a little taller. She'd buried her fear in the pit, and she wasn't letting it out again.

"He has some guts this one, doesn't he?" the warden asked the guards. They laughed and agreed. "Since you like to fight, I'll let you fight Berserker in the arena. Kill two birds with one stone. Get rid of you and make some coins. You know boy, your death will be in vain, that old man died even though you fought so hard to save him. Pity that, but at least I come out on top. It's settled. In two weeks, we will have the event of the year."

Anger washed over her at the senseless death of the old man. The warden could have asked her to slay a dragon in the arena at that moment and she wouldn't have cared, she was too tangled in her emotions. She'd show them that no matter what they put in front of her, she'd come out victorious, including escaping this place.

CHAPTER TWENTY-FOUR

Garret

Garret sat in his room, reading a stolen military report on the current status of Inhous. His hand relaxed, and the report hit his lap as he looked out of the window. Things were getting worse, disease was spreading, and it still hadn't rained.

What could he do? He hadn't the power to make it rain, but there had to be a way to help them. Garret tried thinking of a way to help grow the crops without rain. There weren't any dragons of the dark who knew anything about agriculture, but there had to be someone in the dragons of light. They were all about harmony, but he didn't know any dragons of the light well enough for them to believe he wanted to help the people of Inhous, especially with his father being who and what he was.

A knock pulled Garret from traveling too far down the rabbit hole of helplessness and regret.

"Come in." Garret didn't need to stand to greet his guest. Not when he knew it was Wulf. He was the only person who dared to come to his rooms aside from the servants.

"What can I do for you?" Garret asked.

"My Prince, I have news on a man who is rumored to be one of the best swords in the land. I thought perhaps you would want to take a ride to meet him."

Garret's interest sparked.

"Of course, where is he?"

"In Fergie, about two hours east of here. We could be there and back before anyone misses us."

Garret smiled. Wulf had become someone important to him. Someone who shared his dream for the future and unerringly supported his quests to right his father's wrongs and put a stop to him. Wulf was honorable, a rare quality in a dragon of the dark, but none the less one that Wulf possessed.

Garret stood. "Lead the way"

GARRET AND WULF PULLED their horses to a stop outside the small town.

They dismounted and tied the horses to a tree. Garret ran a hand over King Arthur's nose and pressed his face into his neck.

"Be well, old friend. I will be back shortly."

The horse whinnied. "Good boy," Garret turned toward Wulf. "What is the name of the man we seek?"

"Thomas, the smithy."

"I'm assuming he is a smithy," Garret grinned. Wulf rolled his eyes, and they walked toward town.

AS THEY WALKED, GARRET pulled his cloak over his head to obscure his face from the group of guards at the gate. He didn't believe he would be recognized. Few knew how he looked, but still, he didn't want to draw undue attention when he didn't have to.

Garret and Wulf waited in line as the guards checked each person and their belongings for contraband. As the line moved, Garret and

Wulf heard the taunts of the guards to those who waited to enter the small town. Garret gritted his teeth. Being a dragon of the dark, men being crass or brawling with each other didn't upset or bother him. Petty thefts like a homeless child stealing bread or shoes didn't bother him either. It bothered him when the strong picked on the weak, because there was no value to it.

Garret took a step toward the guards. He hadn't realized he moved until he felt Wulf grab his arm. Garret looked at Wulf. He shook his head. His message was clear. They couldn't be seen. He stepped back and watched the guards. He may not be able to do anything now, but he wouldn't forget these guards. They would get what they deserved. He would see to that.

WITH MINIMAL HASSLE at the gate Garret and Wulf walked through the small town. They passed tents of men and women selling everything from meat to jewelry. A few women stood outside of an inn selling something altogether different.

Soon, they found themselves in front of the smithy. A few customers lingered around, so they waited them out, pretending to look at the daggers and swords. The verdict was still out regarding his swordsmanship, but his ability as a smithy was impressive.

Garret picked up a long sword and held it out. He tested the weight. It was pretty good, but his smithy was better. Two men stood next to Garret, talking. He listened. The best intel was usually overheard.

"It's me day off, and I thought to go to the Palace and have me a drink with a fine lady. I donnae want to waste my coin on buying swords. Let's be off."

The older men shook him off. "Nay, I donnae have the coin to waste on a wench this day. I intend to buy a new sword instead and breastplate. Ye heard what happened at the caves, did ye not? I tell ye, things be changing, and we need to be ready. This be a bad omen, that's what it is, I tell ye true."

"Come now; one person doesn't make an army."

"Nay, but it's not natural."

The younger man laughed.

"Ye laugh, but yer not be laughing when ye lay dead because ye did not kin yer enemy."

The younger man reached up and laid a hand on the older man's shoulder. "Ye make no sense, old man. Come now, ye need a good woman to set ye brain straight. Come now, let's go to the Palace and be treated like Kings."

The older man shook off the younger man, again. "Ye, go alone. I haven't the heart. My heart grows heavy with dread. If ye knew any better, yer heart would too."

"Ye overthink old warrior. I have no more time to waste."

The younger man walked off, Garret put the sword down and moved toward the older man.

"What trouble do you speak of, sir?" Garret asked.

The older man laughed. Garret could see creases on his sun-weathered skin that looked like dried leather. "Nay, I'm no sir," he pointed the direction the boy left. "As the lass said, I'm just an old warrior."

Garret nodded. "And my thanks for your service." The old warrior waved him away.

Garret pretended to look at a few swords in the same area as the old warrior, before asking again. "What trouble were you speaking of? I have a new wife and a babe. If there is trouble arising, I would know so that I can protect my family. Unlike our young friend, I know sage advice when I hear it."

"Ye learned men know how to listen and speak. I'll tell ye cause it's no secret. There be a boy who came out of the pit inside the caves alive. That's never happened before. The pit not be a place ye return from. That pit be where the dragons be born. It shouldn't have happened. It means no good. No good."

"Where is-" Garret was interrupted by the smithy.

"Oy, if ye ain't buying my wares, leave off. I don't give shelter from the sun for free."

The old warrior mumbled his apologies, or he cursed the smithy, Garret couldn't tell, but he walked away from him, and Garret nearly reached out to grab him back. He wanted to know about the pit where dragons were born. He'd never heard of it before, and that's saying something considering he was a dragon, but he held himself. He was here for a reason.

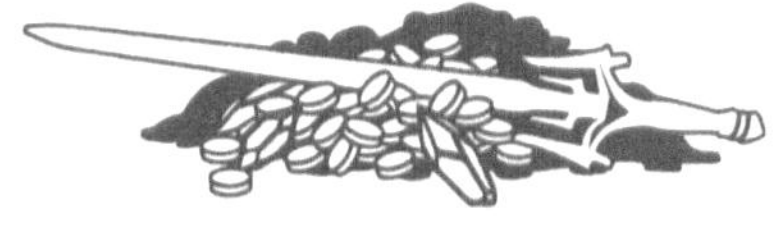

GARRET REFOCUSED ON the task at hand. He walked toward the smithy who stood between him and Wulf, hands folded over his chest, flexing his thickly roped arms, and staring between them. Garret decided to make the first move.

"Have you heard of the tourney that the Emperor is holding?"

"Oy, I've heard of it, so what of it?"

"I've been told you're the best swordsman in the area, perhaps in the land, I just wanted to make sure of it."

"I make swords and wield them, but not for show and not for tha king."

"Emperor," Garret corrected.

"Impostor," the smithy said and spat on the ground.

Garret couldn't argue that. He waved a hand in the air. "That is neither here nor there. What will make you wield your sword? What cause? Or what cost?"

"No cost, whelp, the only cause would be ta free the land from that coward Athel. He dun ruined his lands. His peoples be hungry and diseased. Now he comes here to do the same. I'll not sit back and watch it if I don't be needing ta."

The smithy stood straighter, his relaxed state changed. "Why ye want to know? Ye two work for the imposter?" The smithy was on guard. Perfect. There was no time like the present to find out the truth of the smithy's skill. Garret made his move. Wulf expected Garret to attack and picked up a sword. He threw the sword at the smithy who caught it easily and parried Garret's attack.

Garret stopped and looked at the smithy. His stance wasn't wrong, but it wasn't good either. The smithy absorbed Garret's attacks rather than move to offset it. A man of his stature could do that but not through the entire tourney without tiring. Garret moved back then without hesitation attacked again. The smithy defended, swearing, and calling him names for attacking him without provocation.

The smithy exploded into an attack, yelling at Garret that he'd asked for it. Garret had asked for it. Now, he had to figure out how to end it. The smithy was barreling down on him, pushing his tables out of the way as he came. At least they had more room, Garret thought, but he didn't need it. There wasn't a place that existed where he couldn't fight.

Garret parried the smithy's first attack and noticed how the smithy held the sword. It was all wrong. His hands were too close together; an armature would know better. He was not the best in the land. The waste of time irritated Garret. He glared at Wulf, who shrugged as if to say, how could he have known. Garret gave Wulf a scathing look and finished the smithy with a flick of his wrist that relieved the smithy of his weapon. The smithy was not deterred by the loss of one weapon with more all around him, he went to pick up another, but Wulf was there with a strong hand on the smithy's back. Garret could tell by the expression of pain on the smithy's face that Wulf had a hold of one of those pressure points.

Nasty moves those are.

Wulf applied more pressure, and the smithy's arm went lax. The smithy's jaw clenched tightly. He was trying to fight Wulf's hold. Wulf wasn't going to relent until the smithy relented first. "I wouldn't old boy. We merely wanted to know if you were truly the best."

The smithy struggled, and Garret wanted to tell him it would be better if he relaxed so Wulf would let go, but he didn't think the smithy would be open to his suggestions at the moment. Perhaps he shouldn't have attacked him without at least introducing himself, lie that it would be, but at least he'd have a fake name to curse properly.

Finally, the smithy relaxed and turned his head. "What does it matter to ye who be the best? Ye could have just asked me."

Garret spoke, "If I would have asked you, then you may have lied to me, and I wouldn't know the truth. Everyone believes they are the best, but there's only one person who will be crowned the Emperor's Sword, and that is the person I'm trying to find."

Slowly Wulf eased and let go of the smithy.

"Oy, who will clean this mess?" the smithy asked. Garret nodded his head to Wulf, who handed the man a small leaf of gold, which was enough to buy all the swords in the shop and still have more left. Wulf must like this man to be that generous with his coins.

The sight of the gold quieted the smithy, but not before he grunted a few more curses.

Garret bowed, which was quite the gesture considering his status, but the smithy wouldn't know it. "I apologize for attacking you without provocation, but I wanted to know if the rumors of this area were true. I meant you no harm, and I wouldn't have hurt you, but still, it was rude, and I hope this small amount is enough to compensate for the trouble."

The smithy waved a hand. "Get out! Ye trouble the two of ya. I don't want trouble here."

Garret nodded and Wulf left. Outside, he whispered, "He was barely better than Griffin's squire, who can only hold a sword for five minutes before he gets the shakes. This was not worth the trip."

Wulf shrugged as if to say, these things happen.

"There's a place nearby where we can stop for food," Wulf said.

Exasperated, Garret gestured for Wulf to lead.

"Please, lead the way." Wulf grinned as he walked past him.

THE TWO OF THEM WALKED for a handful of minutes through the town's center. Every once in a while Garret would stop and look at the wares. He found a pair of boots he wanted, but they weren't something he could bring back with him. He would draw the boots and give the picture to Marcus, his shoemaker, to make for him. Knowing Marcus and his flair for the dramatics, the already stunning boots would be even more so.

Garret didn't enjoy many luxuries, but every once in a while, he indulged himself.

"Prince," Wulf whispered, and Garret rolled his eyes.

"If you don't stop calling me Prince, then our little secret mission will be lost. Call me Garret or call me Glorious, but do not call me Prince."

"I'm not calling you Glorious. I will call you Little Sir."

"You better not," Garret commanded sharply.

"Little Sir, up ahead two doors is the place."

Garret squeezed his eyes shut. "I hate you."

"Come on," Wulf said with a lazy smile as they pressed through the crowd.

Wulf turned around, waved him to an open seat. They sat across from each other. Garret inhaled deeply. Both he and his dragon were hungry. His nose processed the different smells, some body odor, ale, roasting meat, and spices but no poisons.

A woman wearing a simple dark green dress with a light green bodice that cinched her waist and pushed her breasts up until he thought they were about to fall out stood in front of them. Garret turned his head to avoid staring directly at her breasts.

"What do ye fine sirs want today?" she asked, her voice husky and filled with promise, which Garret knew was for his benefit or discomfort.

"Two goblets of wine, chicken, bread and fish, enough for us both," Wulf motioned to Garret, who reached back and pulled his hood over his head.

"Pick your head up, Little Sir, there's no threat here," Wulf said.

"I don't know. Her bodice was threatening," Garret said.

Wulf smiled. "Or do you mean tempting, Little Sir?"

"Stop calling me that. I'm a grown man."

"To the humans, but to me, you are a hatchling."

Garret smiled and shook his head. He couldn't deny Wulf was as old as dirt. No one truly knew his origin. The woman came back with the wine. Wulf nodded his thanks. Thankfully, she left as fast as she came. As she did, she passed a table full of men who were too far in their cups. One man reached out and pinched her butt. To Garret's amazement, she pulled back her fist and hit the man in the face. She'd struck him hard enough that he tipped backward in his chair. His head made an awful sound when it hit the floor, and he lay there, out cold.

Garret looked to Wulf, who shook his head and looked down on the man in disgust.

"What was that all about? Women don't hit men."

"They don't in the castle, but things are different depending on where you are, Little Sir. Here, women hit back, so file that away."

"I would never touch a woman who didn't want my touch," Garret said.

"I know. I'm saying file away what you learned today. People and places may look the same, but remember, everyone is different."

"I understand," Garret said somberly.

GARRET LOOKED OVER Wulf's shoulder as the doors to the small eatery were forcible flung open. Garret reached for his sword, prepared to protect himself and those around him, only to relax at the sight of a short slender man wearing vibrant colors of the gentry.

"Where is Monique? Send her to serve me."

The server returned with their food, and Garret nearly forgot all about the man forsaking his curiosity for the pleasures of eating, but his curiosity prevailed, and he asked.

"Ma'am, who is that man?"

"He is nobody, but he believes he is somebody. He comes here and throws around a few bronze pieces, as if they were gold, asks for our best girl, and spends his time speaking loudly about how great he is. A waste of space if you ask me. If given a chance, I'd rather punch him than touch him. Poor Monique has no choice. The beautiful have a heavy cross to bear."

"Thank you," Garret said, and the server left.

Garret reached into the skillet for a chicken thigh, his favorite piece. The chicken slipped off the bone. It was perfectly seasoned. Not too spicy and glazed with just enough honey to make it a bit tangy. *I should recruit the cook.*

"Monique, my dear, you attend me at last. Come, come, spend time with me before I leave to the caves," the gentry said.

The small colorful man continued talking throughout Garret's entire meal. The only time Garret paid attention was at the mention of caves. He'd heard about caves twice in one day, and Garret didn't believe in coincidences. He listened, hoping to get the rest of the information the old warrior didn't say.

Garret tilted his head to look at Monique. She sat on the man's lap. She was beautiful, but her beauty was copied. He'd seen it all before, every day in the halls of the castle. Blond hair, lots of makeup, and perky breasts that were covered with some glowing material. It was annoying, and their perfume cloyed his senses.

"I'd ask you to accompany me, but as you know, these places aren't for ones as delicate as you, my dear. The fights are gruesome and to the death. I will be sitting close enough to the pit that I may even get sprayed with blood. Truly, it isn't for the faint of heart. Only real men like me are even invited this close to the pit. The squeamish men sit farther back. I'll have you know, in my youth, I bested many men, blood is of little concern to me."

Monique oohed and ahhed at all the right times.

The man went on, oblivious to Monique's bored expression.

Garret heard enough. "Wulf, what do you know of this fight and this cave? I've heard of it twice now."

"I haven't heard of it at all before today. Why?"

"I think we should find out about it and attend. The contender is someone that may be of interest to us."

"I will find out more about it."

CHAPTER TWENTY-FIVE

Aquilla

Aquilla woke to another sound kick to the kidneys. She stretched and raised her hands over her head. She opened her eyes and waited for them to adjust to the dim lighting.

"Fox, wake up."

"Go away."

"No, get up."

"No. Go away," Fox said

"Okay, I'll go, but don't blame me for what happens to you next."

Fox sat up. "Shouldn't you worry about yourself? Aren't you the one who has the fight of your life coming up, and no clue how you are going to defend yourself?"

"Muscle memory," she said.

"That's your plan? You are going to put all your marbles on the hope that your body will take over because your mind is blank." Fox stood.

Aquilla's anger built. "You don't get to judge me, Fox. I did what I thought was right. Now, I need to deal with the consequences, and I will. I don't need to explain the how of that to you."

Fox shook his head. "You know Aquillo, at some point, whatever you are working so hard to forget, you will need to sort. You can't live like this forever."

He'd crossed a line. How dare he say she had a hand to play in her memory loss. He knew nothing of how she felt, how she struggled to figure out the missing pieces of her life. Was she a good person or a bad person? Did she have a family waiting for her, looking for her? Or was she an orphan? She wanted to know, but her mind wouldn't give her the answer. He didn't know how it felt to know your own body fought against you, or the fear that she'd never know the truth about her past. Fox was wrong. She wasn't running.

Aquilla's hands balled into fists. The aching pain in her chest intensified. She had to run, so she did. Aquilla ran out of the cave into the tunnel that led to where they worked, but she didn't stop. She blew past the guards into the pitch-black tunnels that would lead her deeper into the cave. She wasn't thinking about where she was going or if she was running off a cliff. The cave was too dark to see anything, much less the ground at her feet or where it dropped off, but she didn't care. Aquilla's fury, frustration, and desperation pushed her forward. She had to outrun her pain.

AQUILLA COULD SEE LIGHT up ahead. She increased her speed, hoping she found a way out. She pulled up short of running headlong into a vast body of water. The light came from an opening far above her head, too far to climb or reach. The sun shone and reflected off the water. Her hopes fell a little because she'd rather have stumbled upon a way out than water. But she couldn't deny the beauty of the place. She sat a little away from the water and closed her eyes. There was a waterfall nearby, and the sound relaxed her and cleared her mind. Her anger disappeared.

Time passed without notice or care. The longer she sat near the water's edge, the more seductive the water became. Aquilla didn't think putting her feet in was a considerable risk. She could easily jump out and run away if she felt something in the water with her. Decided, Aquilla pulled her boots off and dipped her feet into the cool but not cold water. She was surprised when she didn't feel the ground beneath her feet. The depth of the water made her nervous. Still, the sensation of the cool water moving in between her toes and wrapping around her legs felt perfect to a body that had long forgotten the feel of it.

Suddenly, the dirt on her body weighed her down. She needed to bathe. Hiding her sex and bathing had been impossible. The few times they'd allowed them to clean entailed buckets of water being thrown on them one by one. She stayed clothed, convincing others and the guards it wouldn't matter if her body were clean, if her clothes weren't, but at this moment, while nobody was watching, while her mind was at peace, she was free to be herself.

She pulled her tunic over her head and pushed down her trousers. She untied her bindings and pulled off her underwear. Carefully, she placed them in the water. Satisfied, Aquilla sank into the water. She took a deep breath and dunked her entire body under. When her lungs burned, her head broke through the surface. Aquilla gulped in air. She swam a little farther until the sun warmed her skin. Aquilla sighed in relief.

Under the water, she felt something smooth and slippery bump the back of her legs. Without hesitation, Aquilla yelped and swam as fast as she could to her clothes. She scooped them up and swam to the stone surface and jumped out of the water.

How could I be so stupid? Great idea Aquilla to go into unknown water inside a cave with only the gods know what.

Shaking out her wet trousers, she wrestled with pushing her legs into them. When Aquilla lifted her second leg, she froze. A snake coiled itself around her calf. She hopped on one foot, lost her balance, and fell on the damp stone ground.

She thought she'd try reasoning with the snake. "You don't want to bite me, and I don't want you to. I know I was in your water, but there's a lot of water to go around, right?"

The dark blue almost black snake vibrated against her skin emitting a high pitch sound from its scales. Aquilla watched the snake change colors from dark blue to the natural bronze color of her skin.

That's not normal.

She fought the need to peel the snake off. "If you could just unwrap yourself from my leg without biting me, that would be great."

The snake didn't move. It stared at her. Frustrated, Aquilla poked at it, hoping to encourage it to wiggle back to its watery home. She yelped. Lightning-fast the small snake wrapped around her arm from wrist to elbow.

"I should have been more specific. I would like you off my body."

The snake only looked ahead, resting its small head on the middle of her wrist.

"Getting in that water was a terrible mistake," Aquilla said, holding her arm far away from her face.

Aquilla didn't miss the ripples in the water this time, how could she miss a gigantic snake emerging from the water and floating *on top* of it.

"No fear, Aquilla. We buried that in the pit," she reminded herself.

The bigger snake's horizontal pupils turned on her. Aquilla could see the tip of its tongue.

"By the gods," Aquilla said, there's another one? And this one didn't end, or at least, She couldn't see its end. Gently, Aquilla tried to push the little snake off again.

"Go on. Go to the big snake."

"Do not be afraid, little dragon cousin. Neither my son nor I have intentions to harm. It's been a long time since I've seen one of your kind."

Aquilla blinked. *Did the snake just speak? Did it just call me a dragon? And a cousin?*

A human couldn't be related to a snake, and she was human.

"My son likes you."

Aquilla raised her hand and carefully petted the top of the snake's head. Then pushed it a little, trying to dislodge it.

"How is it you can speak?" Aquilla asked.

"Magic, Little Cousin. The same magic that lets you turn into a dragon."

Aquilla ignored the talk of dragons. "Why are you in this cave?"

"For our safety."

Aquilla nodded. "I see. Maybe you can tell him to come back to you? Do I need to put my arm in water so he can swim back to you?"

"My son is in his most troublesome years, between 6000 and 7000 years old. At this age, all kids want adventure, and my son is the same. I could tell him to come to me, but he won't."

"Have you tried?" Aquilla asked.

"I have. He told me no. You know, as a parent, I really don't appreciate the creation of the word, no."

"Are there more of you here, in the cave?"

"There are more here and there." She said vaguely. "Little Cousin tell me, what is the banging about? We hear it, but we dare not get close enough to find out ourselves."

"They are making a city inside the cave, or rather, from the cave, it is hard to explain."

"Who ordered it?"

"I believe Emperor Athel."

"That old fool still lives? And calls himself an emperor no less? Idiot," the large snake sounded annoyed. It switched topics so abruptly the next question took Aquilla off guard. "Who are your parents, Little Cousin?"

Aquilla paused. She tried to pull her parents' names from the ether that blanketed her mind, but none would come to her.

"I don't-I don't remember. I hit my head and lost most of my memories."

"Maybe you can hit your head again, and your memories will come back? Have you tried that?" the large snake asked.

Aquilla shook her head. "That's not something humans can do. It isn't exactly safe."

"Oh, but you aren't human."

"I am!" Aquilla yelled.

"How do you know you are if you can't remember?" The large snake asked.

Aquilla couldn't answer. The talking snake had a point.

"You may have grown up *around* humans. And your parents let you believe you were one of them, but let me assure you, no human can handle a child of mine."

Aquilla looked down at the snake coiled around her arm. She'd nearly forgotten about it.

"You see Little Cousin, my kind are cousins to dragons, better looking, I give you that, but we and the dragons were once bonded. We helped each other survive. My kind ruled the water and dragons ruled the land. My kind can't stay on land for lengthy periods without our bonded dragon, and dragons can't travel the waters without us. So a beneficial kinship was formed many, many years ago."

"I'm sorry, but you are wrong about me. I know it. I may not have my memories, but I'd know if I could turn into a dragon. For starters, I wouldn't be here, trapped in a cave. Maybe your magic is gone because the dragons are gone and now you can attach to humans."

The snake laughed, which sounded more like a long hiss. "Child look at me. Do you think it a trick of the light that I'm floating on top of the water? No, no, my magic is still strong, and you are still a dragon."

Aquilla held up her arm with the snake wrapped around it. "Call your son to you, please. I don't want to be bonded with him. This is all a misunderstanding." She'd had enough of this delusion or dream. She didn't know which, but Aquilla knew she was a human. She bled, starved, and hurt just like any other human.

The water rippled again. Aquilla rolled her eyes.

What now?

Another snake appeared. The small snake on her arm reacted to this one. It hissed at the newcomer who, in turn, laughed.

"What manner of foolishness is this?" the newcomer asked in an unmistakably male voice. This one must be the father.

"Our son has found something he wants to keep," the mother said.

"What is it?" The male moved closer, and its long tongue reached out, barely missing her face.

"Son, don't you dare hiss at me and let go of him, right now. You heard your mother."

"The *human*, dear," the mother said.

"What? He's not human," the father said.

"I've told him this, but he said he is human, denies being a cousin."

"Obviously, dear, he's not well in the mind. One of my cousins told me a story about a dragon who went crazy after breathing in some paste some oddly painted humans gave him. He went mad and couldn't get a hold of himself. He walked straight off a cliff and didn't change. Killed himself, he did. Perhaps he's breathed in the paste too. Son, come here, you don't want the mind-sick dragon. Let it go."

"I am not mind sick, and I'm not a dragon. They don't exist anymore!" Aquilla yelled.

The father snake whispered but neglected to withdraw from her mind. "When they get like this, it's best just to leave them be. Really, there's no saving them from here."

Aquilla screamed. "Get out of my mind. All of you!"

She screamed again until her screams became roars. The snake coiled around her arm, moved up to her neck, then stretched itself down her spine.

Aquilla's senses grew sharper. White scales appeared and disappeared beneath her skin. What was happening to her? She was losing her mind to the delusion.

The father snake tsked. "Crazy as a can of beans, he is. I can't let our son go with something like that. Our son has too much potential."

Aquilla's vision doubled. She didn't have long. Why was she fighting to hold on to this life? She should embrace the darkness, it would be easier, so she did.

CHAPTER TWENTY-SIX

Lilah

Lilah pulled her cloak further down and walked to the city, careful to smear her face with dirt and dress in Duncan's old clothing. Every day, she walked to the city, hoping she would hear something about her granddaughter. She listened for anything about where women were taken. Anything about a girl found in the forest, but she heard nothing. She didn't believe Aquilla was dead, and she wouldn't stop looking for her until she found her.

She stopped at a tent where a woman sold potatoes, tomatoes, and carrots. There were three nicely dressed women standing nearby. Lilah pulled the hood of her cloak lower and listened to the women.

"Have you heard about the crown prince?" A woman wearing a red dress asked her two friends.

"Yes, I've heard he's very good looking and available. My mother wants me to run into him at the tourney accidentally." The woman wearing a pink and blue dress said and winked.

The third woman reached over and grabbed a tomato. She looked at it and gave it a light squeeze, then placed it in the crate. "Well, I heard the crown prince was a snob. He flirts with girls but never asks them out. He's a tease. I've heard the only relationship he has is with the royal library."

"Who cares? When you're as handsome as they say he is, you can do whatever you want. I can't wait to see the long lashes all the girls are swooning over. Do you think they are real?"

Pink and blue dress fanned herself. "Who knows? Does it matter?"

The third woman, who was unimpressed by the prince, said, "I've heard King Daemon will visit during the tourney, and he's bringing his daughter who is rumored to be just as beautiful as the crown prince. There is no doubt the Emperor is trying to play matchmaker."

Two of the women groaned before all three walked away, purchasing nothing.

"Are ye going to be buying that tomato in yer hand?"

It wasn't until the merchant spoke to her that she realized she'd picked it up. She'd clenched the tomato so tightly; juice rolled down her arm. Lilah smiled at the merchant.

"How much?" she asked.

"Three bronze coins and a copper."

Lilah frowned. "That's a little expensive, is it not?"

"Tell it to the Emperor. He keeps raising the taxes, it's getting harder to survive."

"The cruel, greedy man," Lilah said, frowning as she reached into her pocket for the coins.

"It be that way, ma'am. At least King Asthmoth wasn't greedy."

Lilah nodded. "Hopefully, the Asthmoth line will reclaim the throne from this tyrant."

"I very much doubt that, ma'am. There ain't none left."

Lilah shook her head and leaned in closer. She whispered, "I used to work for the royal family, and I saw the queen escape, and so did their hidden granddaughter."

"What hidden granddaughter? And if the queen be living, she best be hiding. That emperor would want her head next to her husband's."

Lilah nodded. "I don't know where she is, but I know the princess learned how to fight when she was young, so she could protect herself and her kingdom when the time came."

It wasn't exactly true, but who would know that but her and Aquilla?

The woman looked at her, really looked at her and asked, "What be the name of this warrior princess?"

"Princess Aquilla Asthmoth, the rightful heir to the throne of the Westlands."

The woman nodded. "I'll be keeping my ear to the ground for the name, but ye still need to pay for the tomato, three bronze coins, and a copper."

CHAPTER TWENTY-SEVEN

Aquilla

"Now, would you look at that? Priscilla is back. I didn't see this plot twist."

"Morgana, Merlin, good to see you both. Is this your son on my back?" Priscilla asked.

"It is," Merlin said proudly.

"How lovely, he will be an excellent friend to my Aquilla."

"Aquilla? That's a girl's name," Merlin said.

"Fitting as my human is a female."

"She looks like a boy," Merlin said, unwilling to move away from the topic.

"Looks can be deceiving, and sometimes deception is necessary. What better way to hide than in plain sight?" Priscilla asked.

"I'll say, I've lived a long time, and I didn't think I'd live to see the day you'd return, but I'm glad for it. How can we aid you, Priscilla? I assume you are here to fulfill the prophecy," Merlin said.

Priscilla sat on her haunches and swung her long white tail around her, skimming the water and splashing Merlin and Morgana.

"My apologies, for that, this spot is a little tight for me in dragon form."

"What of Damascus?" Morgana said.

"My love is here. He came before me. I wanted to find someone worthy to shelter my spirit. I wanted someone who believes in honor and isn't afraid to stand up for what she believes. It took me a while to find someone with such exact qualities, but I was willing to wait. I'll admit, I was becoming anxious that I waited too long and would lose Damascus forever because of it. Then Aquilla's bright light appeared among so much darkness, and I knew she was who I needed."

"She doesn't know it?" Morgana asked.

"No, she was raised with her human father who never told her about her dragon heritage before Athel's men killed him. Aquilla accidentally witnessed the carnage, and she did not take it well. Her mind is somehow broken from it. To make matters worst, she was enslaved and brought here to work in the cave."

"Poor girl," Morgana said.

"Surely she could escape this place if she would only change form. Even now, you could just fly out of here through that big hole up there," Merlin suggested.

"I cannot interfere with her mortal life aside from aiding her in her battles. We have chosen our vessels well. There will be an end and a new beginning, but her life is not mine. I lived my life many years ago. She must live hers no matter what difficulties come from it."

"Sounds unnecessarily complicated to me. You can literally fly out of that hole and be done with it. The one right there." Merlin lifted the tip of his long body to point to the opening, just in case one of them missed it.

"I'm sorry, Priscilla, I think his magic has broken Merlin's mind and to add to that he's male. So you know, forgive him. Please tell us what we can do for you?"

"I would like it if you would let your son stay with Aquilla. And to you Little Cousin on my back, what is your name?"

"Mort," a small voice echoed in the minds of all those in the cave.

Priscilla smiled. He was strong and would suit Aquilla well.

"Mort, I want you to help heal Aquilla's mind. Not too much too fast, but enough so she doesn't continue to break herself at the thought or mention of her past. Is that possible?"

Merlin scoffed. "This is a simple thing for my son to do."

Priscilla nodded her long head in thanks. "Thank you for trusting me with your son. Aquilla and I will protect him with our lives."

Merlin scoffed again. "I'm not worried about my son. He can take care of some little humans. I'm worried he will get hurt protecting Aquilla."

"I see, but you forget. I protect my vessel, so there is no need for your son to do so unless you doubt my abilities..."

"I don't know. When was the last time—"

"Merlin! Enough. Again Priscilla, my apologies, he is truly mind-broken. It should be obvious. We will take our leave now unless you need anything else from us."

"I do not."

"If you need anything, Mort, you know what to do. Enjoy yourself," Morgana said before turning and disappearing under the water. Merlin followed, but not before splashing Priscilla.

"Foolish snake," Priscilla said to Merlin's back, nearly unable to stop herself from going after him. Shaking herself, she stretched her wings. "Mort, hang on, it's time to fly."

The last time Aquilla was this deep into the cave, she flew her as close as possible to the humans before ceding control and waking her up. She'd have to do it again, which could be difficult considering this time, the network of tunnels were far too small to fit her. She'd have to take the longer way over the water to the epicenter of the cave, up those tunnels to the entrance where the humans were.

After some artful flying, Priscilla found a place to land. Sweat sheeted her body. She'd had to maneuver far more than she thought she would have.

"Mort, are you well?"

"Yes, my lady or goddess dragon woman, cousin?"

Priscilla laughed. "My Aquilla calls me Lolanthe. You should call me that too, for now. I will reveal my true name when the time is right. Now, don't forget your job is to heal her broken mind slowly and if she is in a small bind, you can help her out of it, can't you?"

"Yes, Priscilla, I mean, Lolanthe."

"Okay, thank you, Little Cousin. Remember, I was never here. I don't think Aquilla is ready to know about me right now."

AQUILLA AWOKE ONCE again on the ground with no memory of when she walked there.

"You're awake?" A voice said from somewhere or everywhere.

"Who's there?" Aquilla asked and spun around.

"I'm Mort. Son of Merlin and Morgana."

Aquilla used her hands to push herself onto her feet. She looked around for the voice.

"I can't see you?"

"But you can if you look down."

Something squeezed her arm. She couldn't see through in the dark, but she could feel something coiled around her arm. She jumped back, holding it away from her body.

"Don't be afraid. You remember me, don't you? From the water? Overprotective parents? Any of that ring a bell?"

"I remember," she said. "I thought I was dreaming."

"No, you weren't."

"So, what are you?" Aquilla asked, trying to keep calm.

"Let's leave it at a magic snake. I have a few questions. What are you? And why do you look like a boy when you are a girl, because I didn't see any male human bits in the water."

Aquilla was mortified. "Be quiet. What did you see in the water?"

"No human boy bits, but I did see girl ti-"

"Stop! Don't finish that. Don't mention it. Don't breathe a word of it to anyone. I'm disguised as a boy for reasons of convenience. You will figure it out soon."

"What's your name?"

"Aquilla. Will it hurt you if I put my arm down?"

"No. I can't feel anything like this. I do feel what you feel, but that's not so much physical as metaphysical."

"I don't know what that means," Aquilla said and walked forward.

"You will figure it out soon. I like you," Mort said.

"Glad to hear it. How are you talking to me? I feel like you are everywhere in my mind."

"I am speaking to you inside your mind. You can speak to me this way too. That's all a part of the metaphysical thing I mentioned. Don't worry. You'll get it."

Aquilla rolled her eyes. She wasn't a child. "What kind of magic snake are you?"

"My father, Merlin, is a direct descendant of Jörmungandr, also known as the Midgard Serpent. My mother, Morgana, is a direct descendant of Tiamat, which is why, for a while, she was a little bloodthirsty, before my father tamed her."

"He tamed her?"

"That's what my father told me. He said with women you have to tame them because they are wild beasts. Once they are tamed, you can talk sense to them. My father is rarely wrong about anything."

"Oh, he's definitely wrong about that."

"I seek to tame you," Mort said.

Aquilla laughed. "I don't think so."

"We'll see. My father taught me everything," he replied. Aquilla ignored him and kept feeling her way back. "Do you come off?" Aquilla slowed down as she reached the entrance to the cave that depressingly held her hostage.

"I can't. If I'm not connected to either water or your body, I will die."

"Die?"

"Yes, cease to exist. Is there another meaning for the word?"

"No, but how will this work? I can't feed you when I don't have food for myself. I can't do anything for you," Aquilla said, defeated with her situation.

"Don't worry, as long as you're alive, I am too," Mort said.

"Well, Mort, you are welcome to stay on my arm as long as I have one," Aquilla said, then walked into the cave and waited for the guards to come. Her second return would earn her another visit with the warden.

CHAPTER TWENTY-EIGHT

Aquilla

Two weeks passed in a blur of hard work during the day and thoughts of her future at night. Every day the guards mocked her, told her she was as good as dead, and every day she ignored them, fighting the temptation to hit them, but them mocking her was far less harmful than what they did to others. Day after day, she watched as they beat the other workers. Day after day, she and the other workers ate food that held no value to their health. Rapidly, the men around her weakened in body and spirit.

Enough. It was all enough. Someone had to do something, and that someone was her. A plan formed in her mind, one that might get her killed, but what did she have to lose? Fox interrupted her musings.

"Are you awake, Aquillo?"

"Yes, why are you awake so early?" she asked.

"I don't know. I was thinking about the fight tonight."

"What about it?"

"You can win, right? I mean, you will win, right?"

"I'll do better than that, Fox."

"What does that mean?"

"I'm not staying here another night, and neither are you."

"Be smart, Aquillo. Don't do anything that will put you at risk."

"Fox, I can't remember my past. I can't remember if I'm a good or bad person, but I do know, without a doubt, I won't stand for this in-

135

justice anymore. If the other men are too broken or afraid to find a way out, then I will find a way for them."

Silence fell between them for a few minutes before Fox said, "If you find a way out, then I will follow you, Aquillo."

AQUILLA STOOD IN LINE behind Fox as she did every morning. They waited for the guards to walk them to breakfast or gruel fuel as Aquilla began calling it. One guard broke away and walked down the line. He stopped in front of her.

"I thought for sure you would jump off the cliff during the night to avoid a far worse death by Berserker's hands tonight," the guard said.

Aquilla glared at him. "That would mean I'm afraid, which I'm not."

"You will be, but as a boon, the warden is giving you special treatment today. You, boy, will get three meals of real food, not this slop you've been eating, a bath, and some clean clothes. Come with me."

Aquilla stepped out of line and followed the guard, all the while, trying to control her impulse to push him over the cliff's edge.

"Turn left here, boy."

"My name is Aquillo. A.QUILL.O"

"I don't care what your name is because, after tonight, you won't ever hear it spoken again."

"That's what you think," Aquilla said.

THE GUARD STOPPED IN front of a large orange wooden door and opened it. Aquilla thought more work went into building the warden and the guard's rooms than the actual city within the cave the Emperor asked for. She wondered what would happen to the warden if the Emperor were to find that out.

When Aquilla walked into the scarcely decorated room, the first thing she noticed was the bed. The second was the wooden tub off to the right. If someone was going to watch her bathe, that would be a problem, but then again she had Mort and he had magic.

The guard searched the room. He didn't find anything. "Don't try to escape. I'll be standing right outside this door."

Aquilla rolled her eyes. "I'm not going anywhere."

"You got that right," he said, slamming the door behind him.

Aquilla walked to the bed and fell on to it. The bed was soft against her back. It was a luxury she hadn't had for as long as she could remember.

"Mort," Aquilla called in her mind.

"Yes."

"If someone were to come in while I was bathing, could you magic them to think I was a boy? You know, give me boy bits?"

"Easy, we could also just, I don't know, kill the guy. Might be easier."

"No, no, none of that. I don't think I'm a murderer."

"But wouldn't it be interesting if you were?" Mort asked.

"I don't think it would be. It sounds like an awful life to live."

"Maybe they weren't innocent. Maybe they deserved it," Mort said.

"Nobody deserves to be killed by me."

Aquilla's eyes grew heavy with sleep. Cocooned by the soft bed, Aquilla drifted to sleep. If Mort said more, she didn't hear it.

AQUILLA LOOKED AROUND. She was on a mountain. She looked down at the view below. A man and a little girl practiced fighting.

"Hold your fist like this and rotate it palm down on the punch. Sink a little more and widen your legs before you throw the punch."

"Yes, Father. Like this?"

"Perfect, my little Lily."

Aquilla moved closer. The girl looked familiar. She was watching a younger version of herself, so that meant the man with his back toward her, helping her with her punches, was her father. She had someone out there waiting on her—someone who loved her enough to teach her how to protect herself. Aquilla wanted to see his face. She walked around to stand behind her younger self. She looked into her father's hypnotizing green eyes. She saw love and pride in their depths. Her father's brown hair was tied into a topknot like hers. Aquilla reached out to touch his face, feel the beard he'd grown. Her hand waited suspended in the air as time spun around her day after day blurred past her. Aquilla watched her younger self grow taller and stronger until time stopped, and she faced herself.

"You need to wake up and remember," her twin self said.

"Why? I want to stay on the mountain with you and father."

"You can't."

"Why can't I?" Aquilla pleaded.

"Because you have something important to do."

"Nothing is as important as my family."

"Yes, it is. Many people are depending on you to lead them out of the darkness and into the light."

"I don't have anything to do with that. Where's Father?" Aquilla asked, looking over her twin's shoulder. *"I want to see him again."*

"You can't."

"Stop telling me I can't. I can do whatever I want."

Her twin self shook her head. *"You can't raise the dead."*

"What do you mean?"

"Father was killed by the Emperor's men when he conquered King Asthmoth's land. Remember."

"No, I don't want to. I don't want to remember that."

"You must!" her twin demanded. "We aren't weak. We are strong and brave. That's what father taught us, and you do not honor his memory by behaving as you are. You are but a shade of your real self. You have to remember."

Aquilla shook her head. She couldn't do it. She didn't want to do it. She took several steps back.

"Go away," Aquilla yelled at her twin. In a move faster than she could see, her twin grabbed her arm and pulled her down the mountain. Aquilla didn't know where she was being pulled. Panic bubbled up, and she grabbed trees and branches. She dug her feet in, but nothing slowed them. Then she saw Fox barking at her.

She moved him out of the way and ran. Her twin pulled her, forcing her to watch herself fight.

"Look at yourself fighting. What do you see?"

Aquilla closed her eyes. She didn't want to see anymore. It was too much.

"Open your eyes, Aquilla, and look."

She opened them.

"Tell me, what do you see? What did you do wrong?"

Aquilla watched herself fight soldier after soldier. She swung her sword wildly using her strength and no skill at all. Tears flowed down her eyes, and grief marred her expressions.

"Wild. I was wild."

"Why?" her twin asked.

Aquilla steeled her heart and kept watching and thinking. "Because I let my emotions control the fight, something I should have never done."

"Exactly. This type of fighting will get you killed, and you have more to do. Look at me."

Aquilla turned to look at herself.

"We are meant for greatness in this world, but not for us but others. We can't allow our emotions to get in the way of our battle. Our enemy has *a name. Athel. He is responsible for our father's death, and he torments our people. We have a clear purpose. But this Aquilla, this wild unskilled fighting will get you killed long before you avenge our father, long before you set our people free. Remember this. No matter what, control your feelings. Don't be afraid to get in the zone. Now wake and fight to win."*

The grin on her twin's face was one she could relate to—the joy of a fight to come.

THE SMELL OF FOOD GREETED her when she woke. She sat up in bed and looked around. Clean clothes sat on the foot of the bed.

"Finally, you're awake," Mort said.

"Yes, more than you know."

"Great, can we eat that? It smells delicious. It's real meat."

Aquilla grinned. She picked up a thigh bone and took a large bite. The meat was tender and juicy. How they managed that in a cave, Aquilla would never know. As she ate, her mind turned to the plan she'd made earlier then to her new enemy. If Emperor Athel thought he'd conquered her land, he was wrong, and she would show him exactly how wrong it was to bring his army into her backyard. But first, she had to win the fight tonight.

Bring it.

She may not have remembered herself until now, but her recent experiences taught her something important. Evil filled the world, and good people had no one to protect them, and women weren't considered much more than bearers of children. Aquilla would protect the people who couldn't fight for themselves, and it would begin tonight, because her strength and memory came together.

CHAPTER TWENTY-NINE

Garret

Garret and Wulf slipped into the tunnels and walked toward the arena. They were dressed as guards, so they could stand in the front, right at the edge of the arena. Garret wanted to see close up if the boy spoken about everywhere would live up to expectations. Even though, he held on to a slither of hope, he braced himself for another disappointment. Time was running out and worry pricked him. If he couldn't find a suitable swordsman, his plan would fail, and he'd miss this opportunity. How long would it be before he'd have another chance to bring his father down? How many people would have to die before that chance came? Garret shook off his morose thoughts, he had to hope, if not this boy, then another man was out there, and he'd find him in time.

CHAPTER THIRTY

Aquilla

There was a knock.

"Boy, are you ready?" The guard asked for the third time.

Aquilla opened the door. "Lead the way."

He grunted and motioned for her to follow him. She was calm. Her body was relaxed, and she was confident in her ability. She'd trained a lifetime for this.

The guard walked her up to the entrance and pushed her inside.

The intense light from the lamps and the heavily scented men and women overwhelmed her senses. The sounds were too loud after weeks, maybe months, of silence. When she looked into the crowd that circled her, she saw sights she'd never seen before. The women's faces were pale from white powder. Instead of binding their breasts so nobody else could see them, these women pushed them up and wore them out in the open. Both the men and women's clothes were filled with brightly colored patterns.

Her mind reeled back to her reality when the crowd began booing her as she walked further onto the arena.

There were rows and rows of people watching her. Taunting her. A thin layer of sand felt like grit under her feet. The warden walked onto the arena floor. His voice boomed.

"Joining us tonight is Aquillo, the boy who survived the pit not once but twice! He may look scrawny but let me assure you this fight will be well worth your coins and time."

Aquilla stood looking at the warden in disgust. Then she turned her glare on the crowd. These people were awful. They came to see her, and a man fight to the death. What was wrong with them? Was there not enough death the night Emperor Athel conquered the land?

A thickly roped man with an ax and a bad attitude walked toward the warden. When his eyes landed on Aquilla, she saw something unexpected. Pity.

Interesting.

"And here he is, our reigning champion, Berserker!"

The crowd cheered. Some were yelling for him to kill and others to make her death quick and painful.

"These people aren't making it easy to want to be a good person to them, are they, Mort?"

"Indeed, I would like to give them a thrashing myself," Mort responded. Having Mort coiled around her arm gave her a sense of security and grounded her. If nobody else was on her side in this whole place, Mort was there fighting with her.

The warden pushed her to one side and Berserker to another before he moved out of the arena. A bell of sorts sounded, and Berserker exploded out of the corner, running at her with an ax in hand. Funny how they neglected to give her a weapon.

Aquilla dodged his first strike but didn't move in time to avoid the kick to her stomach. Her breath caught a bit before she rolled out of the way of his next strike that would have placed his foot deep in her gut had she not moved. Aquilla stood then dropped into her fighting stance, legs bent, hands up and waited. While she waited, Berserker played to the crowd giving them battle cries and throwing his arms in the air.

Aquilla debated the honor in striking him with his back turned from her. She argued with herself that they were in the middle of a fight. He had to know she would hit him, but she waited because there was no honor in striking an opponent from behind. Once Berserker was done. She ran straight at him.

He struck out, intending to bury his ax in the middle of her head, but she moved to the left and used his momentum to pull him down and punch him in the face. Berserker swore. Blood poured from his nose. He ignored it and swung his ax again, this time attempting to take her head off shoulders, but she ducked then jumped up and punched him in the side of the head. He wobbled on his feet. Aquilla didn't hesitate. She kicked the ax from his hand, spun, and kicked him again on the side of his head. Berserker went down too close to his ax. Aquilla slid and grabbed it. The crowd was stunned silent, Turning Aquilla straddled Berserker with his ax at his throat.

Sounds of disgust and cries of foul play echoed inside the cave. The warden marched toward her, stopping just outside her reach.

He yelled at her, demanding she kill Berserker as the rules stated. Instead, Aquilla bent down and whispered in Berserker's ear, "I'm not going to kill you, nod if you understand."

He nodded.

"Good, I'm going to get out of here, nod if you want to go with me."

Slowly, he nodded, again.

"I'm going to stand now, but you stay down."

Aquilla stood, ax in hand. The warden stepped back. She smiled, channeling her Fox from the forest, all teeth and menace, which only scared the warden more. He took several steps back.

Good. It's my turn now.

She never took her eyes off the warden when she addressed the crowd. "You all came here to watch two men try to kill each other for fun? You are morbid, and your morality is corrupt. Do you think

Berserker, or I volunteered for this? Do you think we will get some compensation for fighting and killing each other? We won't! And you won't get what you want tonight either! There will be no bloodshed."

The crowd began to murmur and demand their coins back. The warden found his anger.

"Give me the ax, you troublesome boy. Hand it over before I call my guards to come take it from you by force."

The crowd was leaving by the droves, and the rage in the warden's eyes made it plain. If she didn't figure out how to get out of this cave tonight, she would be very sorry. Good thing she had a plan.

AQUILLA GRABBED THE warden and put the ax to his throat. Some nobles who were still seated watched the sight unfold with giddy excitement. Aquilla ignored the fools.

The guards ran to protect the warden, but they were too late.

"Unhand me, boy."

"Aquillo. My name is Aquillo, and no, I won't. Here's what's going to happen. Tonight, you are going to help me set the men free. Once they are free, I will let you go."

"I will do no such thing! The Emperor himself put me in charge, and he would have my head if I failed him!"

"So, your options are to die by my hand or his?"

The warden was silent.

"If I were you, I would put your faith in me because if you do what I have asked, you will live. With your connections, I'm sure you could hide in the North or South Lands. I don't believe the Emperor has conquered those lands, yet. So what do you say?"

Aquilla drew a little blood so he knew she wasn't kidding, and to her surprise, she realized she wasn't. She would kill him if he didn't comply. Her willingness to do so disturbed her on several levels she'd have to dissect later. "Decide warden. Me or the Emperor. Life or certain death." Aquilla pushed the blade of the ax a little deeper.

"You. You!" He yelled to the guards. "Free the men. Free them all."

Aquilla's heart soared. She wanted to shout victory, but there was still more to do. She pulled the warden with her and yelled for Berserker.

"Berserker, you can get up now."

Berserker nodded. Aquilla turned to the guards.

"I need three of you to help me, so who will it be?"

Most of the guards ran out the door without looking back, leaving the warden to figure out his future himself. More than three were still deciding. Aquilla added some motivation. "Don't make me have my friend Berserker pick."

Three men stepped forward, and the others left. "Okay, you three, lead the way, but first, let's make a stop to wherever you are holding the coin from tonight's fight. I think my friends are owed a little coin for their troubles."

The guards nodded and walked forward. At the last minute, Aquilla changed her mind. "Berserker, you're taller than me. You hold the warden."

The warden struggled from her grip, but Berserker caught him by the throat and looked him in the eye. "I never liked you," he said before circling the warden, ready to take the warden's head off if he gave him the slightest chance.

Aquilla brought up the rear as they all followed the guards in the front. They stopped in the throne room as Aquilla liked to call it and picked up a closed glass case full of coins, mostly gold. Aquilla told one guard to carry it. She needed both hands free to fight if it came to that.

They moved from one tunnel to the next before they reached the dimly lit cliff ledge where the men slept.

"Wake them," Aquilla said, never leaving Berserker's back unprotected. A deal was a deal, and he was holding up his part so she would too. When all the men gathered, Aquilla instructed Berserker to put his back against the wall so she could speak.

"I know it is early to wake, but tonight I have a gift for you. Your freedom and coins to get you started in your new life. I suggest you flee this land for North or South so you can live freely. If you are here because you committed a crime, here is your chance for a new beginning, a better beginning. If you have a family, I suggest you settle yourself before you send for them. If you are afraid for their safety, wait until the morning, and I will help you get them to safety."

"I will help too," said Fox from within the crowd.

"As will I," said another voice she hadn't expected to stick around long after his debt was paid. She turned and nodded her thanks to Berserker and continued.

"Right now, we will follow these guards out of the cave. Fox, come here." Carefully, he made his way to her side. She clapped him on his shoulder. "Go get that glass box from that guard," Aquilla pointed to the second guard standing next to the guard who led them back to the men. "And come back," she said loud enough for all to hear, "The guard will give you the glass box because he doesn't want to die tonight."

Fox nodded and made his way to the guard and back. "Let's go. Lead the way, guards."

Aquilla hustled Berserker and the warden to the front of the line a half an hour later. She felt fresh air kiss her skin. Freedom. The men were overcome with happiness. They clapped each other on the back and shook hands. Many hugged her. She wanted to give them time to deal with their new reality, but they just didn't have the time. There was no doubt in her mind the Emperor would soon find out about their escape and send someone after them.

"Men, go to Fox, get your coins, and start moving north or south as fast as you can. I have no doubt the army will be here soon. Hurry, everyone."

After receiving their coins, some men ran the wrong way, not knowing east from west or north from south, but Aquilla couldn't worry about every detail. She did her best. Some stayed around asking for her help with their families. Berserker held firm to the warden, and two of the three guards stayed and helped those who were turned around, find their way north, or point them south. Aquilla smiled. Perhaps all these guards needed was an opportunity to do good.

Once the last person either ran or stayed, Aquilla turned to the warden and the guards. She gave the warden two gold coins because she promised him life, and she meant it, but she gave the guards three gold coins because they weren't forced to remain here, they did so on their own. Aquilla looked at the box. There was still more than enough for Aquilla, Fox, and Berserker.

Aquilla watched as the warden waddled away, tripping over a stone in his hurry. She promised him life, but the other men made no such promise. Hopefully, they would show him mercy. She turned to the remaining group, shocked to see the guards still there in the back, watchful and listening. Three men said their families needed protection. Aquilla didn't know how she could protect them and smuggle them out of the kingdom, but she would try because she promised and her father's constant lessons on honor and to protect the weak were all she had left of him. She wouldn't let him down by throwing those lessons away for an easy escape.

"Aquilla, whatever you are going to do, you need to do it fast. I sense a group coming our way quickly," Mort said.

"Can you tell how many?" Aquilla asked.

"I don't know, but too many for us to take in our current condition."

"Which way should I go? North or south?" she asked.

"South," Mort answered.

Everyone stared at her. She smiled. She'd have to do better with her private conversations with Mort, or she'd be called mad.

"Follow me," she said and took off south.

INTERLUDE TO DARKNESS

A **Thousand Years Earlier**

The council assembled to pass judgment on him. What had he done wrong? Nothing. He followed his instincts and did what had to be done. It wasn't his fault these pious dragons didn't have the forethought he did. Valin looked up at the council members who sat above him with their noses held high.

How was it Priscilla and her lover Damascus were given seats on the council before him? They were nothing, but now, they judged him? Never.

His brother Lucian spoke first. His original keeper.

"Brother, I have tried for so long to get you to see reason. We are dragons. Our base instincts push us to crave treasurers, but we have to be stronger than our baser instincts if we are to exist at all. Who can have it all? What would that mean? The dragon who has it all will tear the world apart to get it. We can't let that happen. We have a responsibility to the dragons who look to us for protection."

Valin laughed. "Who looks to us? Who worships us? These two hatchlings?" He pointed to Priscilla and Damascus. "No, not once have I heard of them doing anything in your name. We are forgotten, gods. I only want the power and acknowledgment we deserve."

Lucian's fist hit the marble table. "We are not here to rule the dragons. We are here to help them!"

Valin sneered. "We are gods. We were made to rule!"

"No, we were made to serve!" Lucian yelled.

"I serve no dragon. Why would I? My power is immense. What would be the point? They will serve me, you, all of us if we choose. You all stay hidden in the clouds. Only interfering when we couldn't be seen. Why? Is it because of our Great Dragon Father? He hasn't been seen or heard from in thousands of years. It's time we start making our own decisions."

"You are wrong, Valin. Just because our Great Father hasn't been seen, that doesn't mean we should forget his lessons. At some point, every parent leaves their child to live their own life hoping the values they were taught were good enough. Our Great Father gives us his trust so he can rest. For so long, he carried the burden alone. Now, when his children are here to help, we almost destroy everything he worked to build. You were wrong, Valin. You should not have influenced the dragons to evil."

Valin crossed his arms over his chest. "I didn't exactly influence them to evil. I made some suggestions, and they decided on their own they were worth doing. I can't help that darkness lives inside us all."

Damocles put a hand on Lucian's shoulder, stopping him from speaking further. "Valin, our Great Father gave you the most difficult job of us all. He gave you the job to keep balance, to be the dark to Lucian's light. We thought maybe you needed a break. Maybe you needed to step back for a while, but you assured us you were fine when you weren't. Now, it has come to this. Your plans to spread your darkness caused an imbalance that cost Priscilla and Damascus their lives. If you hadn't played both sides, one of the Kings would have saved them and ushered in the next era. Your actions have created a devastating effect on the future of dragons. Even us gods aren't sure where to go from here."

Annoyed, Valin spoke. "Damocles, shut up. Nobody wants to hear you. What? Are you mad that I ruined the little love fest you made? Get over yourself. The powerful gods are speaking," Valin said.

Lucian rose. "Enough, Valin, I sentence you to a fate of your creation. I sentence you to perpetual darkness. Without shape or form. Without light or joy. You, brother, need a taste of how it feels to be surrounded by darkness so you understand why you can never rule Earth. Damascus and Priscilla are your keepers. I don't trust that you will lie down and take your punishment. I trust you will find some way to free yourself, and when that happens, Damascus and Priscilla will be there to stop you. As for the rest of us." Lucian looked around. "We rest. We are of no help to our dragon family now. They don't need gods; they need friendship, but the gods can't fully disappear so we will leave things to Damascus and Priscilla. They will watch over the Earth day and night. Priscilla, Damascus, I will not leave you alone in this task. Our snake cousins will know you and help you along the way. You have but to call upon them."

Valin laughed. "You think these two are enough? Do you think they are stronger than me? Don't make me laugh, brother."

Lucian looked amused. Valin shifted in his seat. His brother was up to something.

"I will be the example for you to follow. I will give my power to Priscilla."

There was an audible gasp from several other gods. "Don't try to dissuade me. I know what I'm doing. I will go to Earth to live among our brothers and sisters and die as the Great Father sees fit. I will be an example. For as long as I breathe, I will work to right your wrongs, Valin."

Lucian held his hand out palm up and slowly closed it. Valin felt Lucian's power as he pulled it from him. Valin looked at Priscilla. She smiled. Her lips were moving. She was telling him something. Valin gripped his heart. He leaned in. Darkness closed around him, his darkness. Then he realized what Priscilla said.

"Come get some."

CHAPTER THIRTY-ONE

The Deal

Aquillo ran, and Garret followed him, staying close behind to make sure the older men in the group were't left behind. He knew soon if not already, his father would send his men to the caves. Not because he remembered or cared, but an escape was an insult to his power. He wouldn't let that go.

He hoped they would all make it to safety before his father's men caught up with him because Garret didn't know if the older men could keep going at this speed. Garret looked up. The moon was high in the sky, moving fast to cover the vast distance around the world. He and Wulf would need to shift to their dragon forms to return to the castle before morning. They needed to hurry.

They slowed as they entered the forest. The man named Fox led them. Once they found a safe place to camp for the night. Garret listened for the sound of soldiers following. He heard nothing, but just in case he turned to Wulf and nodded. Wulf understood what Garret wanted without speaking words, and he ran off to scout. Now, Garret needed to find a way to speak to Aquillo alone.

He could only imagine how Aquillo felt with so many asking him to do the impossible. The thought of adding to his burdens bothered him, but he had to do it. He had to make a deal with Aquillo tonight, or he may never see him again, and the thought of losing this opportunity was more than he could handle. It bothered him on a level deeper than it should have; it shook his spirit.

Strange, but he didn't have time to think about it. He had a job to do. Aquillo was the man he'd been looking for. He had to talk to him. He had to get him on his side and to the tourney, somehow.

Garret looked around. He found Aquillo helping the men settle for the night. Garret joined him. He was their crown prince, after all. He stripped out of the guard clothes and walked into the makeshift camp. The men were afraid of him. He could only imagine what happened to them in those caves. He went to each man and asked how they were and apologized for his actions. While he may have done nothing, his father caused their pain, and he had done nothing to stop him.

Garret walked up to Fox and Aquillo, who sat next to each other on a log. He stood in front of Fox and held his hand out. He saw mischief and recognition in his eyes.

"Don't we already know each other?" Fox asked.

"No, I don't believe we've ever met, but I admit you seem familiar," Garret said.

"I felt the same way when I met Fox," Aquillo said. "It's funny because when I met Fox, I couldn't remember my past. Now that I have my memories back. I remember I had a fox that I named Fox, and we played together in the forest." Garret noticed she trailed off toward the end of her sentence as if it pained her to think of her past, but then a memory of his own surfaced. He knew a girl who had a fox named Fox who played in the forest. Garret looked closer. The details of Aquilla's face had blurred over time, but one thing he'd never forgotten was her hazel eyes. The same eyes Aquillo had. Before he could speculate about the relationship between Aquilla and Aquillo, Fox stood and placed a hand on Garret's shoulder. He bent down and whispered. "This Fox and that Fox are one in the same, dragon boy. Dragons aren't the only predator squatting on this planet."

Garret's eyes widened. He had so many questions, but now wasn't the time. He looked at Aquillo again, his eyes, face, and hair. Could it be this was Aquilla? It was possible. She'd worn clothes fitting of a boy all those years ago. Aquillo shifted under Garret's intense gaze, and with that, he knew. This man wasn't a man at all. First, his heart fell. He couldn't send a woman to do a man's job. He couldn't send her to fight his father, but she'd just fought a relative giant and won. Could she do it? Garret didn't have much choice. His feelings warred within, but his responsibility to his people won out. He had to stop his father, and male or female Aquilla was his best chance.

Aquilla and Garret were alone. He didn't know how to start. Thankfully, Aquilla spoke first.

"You shouldn't lie to people, you know. It isn't honorable."

"What did I lie about?"

"You said you would help us get the men's families out of the city. I doubt our once ruthless keeper would become our ally so easily."

"I wasn't lying. I will help you help them," Garret said defensively. How could she think he'd lie about something so important? Then again, she thought him one of the guards that kept them captive.

"Are you doing this for penance?" Aquilla asked.

"I didn't want to do any of the things that I had to do to the men in the cave. It was the order of the Emperor. I didn't want to die because I defied the crown. Aquillo, you know how cruel Athel can be. I was a coward. I understand how trusting me would prove difficult, but please try. I only want to help make things right."

"I hate him," Aquilla said with disgust.

"Who?" Garret asked.

"The Emperor. He and all those who follow him are careless with human life."

Garret flinched.

Aquilla continued. "I won't let the Emperor get away with killing and capturing people without cause. It isn't right. His ruthless attitude is passed down through his ranks, leaving many without morals or values and encouraged to be just as ruthless as their ruler. He must be stopped, and I've signed up to do the job."

Hope soared within Garret. She already shared his vision and understood him. That would make things easier. All Garret needed to do was introduce the idea and let the conversation move naturally. A twang of guilt betrayed his determination, but Garret fought past it. He had his reasons.

"How do you plan to stop him?"

"I don't know, but I'm resourceful. I will find a way."

"What about the tourney open to all to find the best swordsmen in the lands? The winner is crowned the Emperor's Sword. That will get you close to the Emperor, close enough to take your vengeance. Close enough to save our land from a tyrant."

Aquilla shook her head. Garret panicked. "Why?" he asked, trying, and failing to keep the plea out of his voice.

"I won't be a coward and use deception as a way to face my enemy. I want to meet him in battle. Face to face."

Garret's panic subsided. "What if you win the tourney and then call him to fight you, right there?" Garret suggested.

"Would he? Or would he laugh and kill me outright?"

Garret had no doubt his father would fight a little human. If for no other reason than to show the other humans, why they should fear him. "I have met him and worked for his family. From everything I know about him, I have absolutely no doubt he would accept your challenge. The question is, are you strong enough to take him on?"

Aquilla didn't hesitate. "How do I enter?" she asked.

Garret should be happy. He came here to find the best swordsman. He came here to get that person to work with him against a common enemy. Garret should be happy, over the moon. He was closer than ever before. His father would finally meet his match, and if Aquilla couldn't finish him, Garret would. So why did he feel so low? Why did he feel horrible? And he wasn't finished.

"I can help you. I know we aren't exactly friends, but like you, I have my reasons for helping."

Aquilla perked up. "And what are those reasons?"

At least here, he could be honest. "He's too destructive. The people in the kingdom are suffering, and he doesn't care. He overtaxes the merchants who raise their prices, and most people can't afford food. They are starving. It isn't right."

Aquilla used her foot to push dirt around. "If you felt this strongly, then why did you become a guard? Why did you work against us in the cave?"

"I can't fight alone, and I have responsibilities I can't forsake. There were so many days I wanted to raise my sword and fight, but my responsibilities forced me to be strategic, so I waited for someone like you."

"How can you help me?" Aquilla asked.

"I can find you a sponsor and help you train. I never said I wasn't good at fighting, just that I couldn't fight alone."

Aquilla looked Garret in his eyes and held his stare. She flayed him open, uncovering his secrets and desires until they all lay open for her judgment. Her hazel eyes pierced his soul and warmed his body. His dragon stirred. Aquilla broke eye contact first.

She cleared her throat. "Before I do anything, I have to help these men's families. They are my first responsibility."

"I agree," Garret said, "But that doesn't mean we can't train while we figure out how to help them, right?"

Aquilla turned her face toward the skies in thought. The moon washed over her; she was radiant under the light. How could he have ever thought she was a he?

Without looking back at him, her eyes stayed trained on the skies. She said, "Okay, it's a deal. You figure out all the tourney details, and I will figure out how to get the families out of the city unnoticed. In between that, we can train and plan."

Garret noticed how soul-tired she appeared. What happened to her? How did she end up here? Instinctively, he knew now wasn't the time to ask.

"Okay, I need to head back tonight to keep suspicion down. I will meet you in the town square at noon. My name is Garreth, and my friend and our ally Wulf will be there as well. You can bring Fox and Berserker if that will make you feel comfortable."

She snorted. "I will bring them because I think they would feel more comfortable. I'm not afraid of anything, because I have nothing to fear."

Garret stood. They'd struck the deal.

AFTER GARRETH LEFT, Aquilla waited a while, taking in all that happened over the last few months and all that was to come. She would avenge her father's unfair death and all those like him. She would protect all those who suffer under the Emperor or die trying.

"Aquillo!" Fox called, holding up an orange under a tree. His white teeth shone through the night like a beacon welcoming her home. Aquilla stood. Life was becoming interesting.

CHAPTER THIRTY-TWO

Friend or Foe?

The next day, Aquilla set the men on their way and noted who was going where to send their families to the correct destination. Now, she set off to the last place she wanted to be, but the only place she needed to be, the capital. Fox, Berserker, and Aquilla took the off road moving around trees in and out of shaded areas. They were currently walking through a field of tall grass. The grass reached her knees. The sun beat down on them. Her skin burned and sweat dripped down her back. The sweat rolled down her chest, making her bindings uncomfortable. She needed shade and to bathe, but there wasn't anything she could do but keep moving forward.

Aquilla turned around to see how her fellow travelers fared. Berserker kept to his word and vowed to see everyone safe, including Aquilla, or Aquillo, as he called her. Berserker had taken his shirt off and wrapped it around his bald head. Aquilla wished she could do the same, but then she'd be exposed for the woman she was, and questions about Mort would ensue, both of which she didn't want to talk about.

Fox walked with his head up, face drawn in thought. Aquilla wanted to know what put the wrinkles between his eyes.

"I think there is a town up ahead. We should be able to buy horses and a bed for the night. Maybe even bathe," Berserker said.

Aquilla's spirits lifted. "Great. Let's make haste. I could use a bath."

IT TOOK ANOTHER HOUR of walking to get to the town. They spent half of that time walking through the open field of grass. Once there, Fox took charge, which Aquilla was grateful for. She hadn't remembered ever feeling so exhausted or hungry. Not even when she was starving at the caves.

"Berserker, you find out if we can buy some horses. I refuse to walk all the way back to the capital. I mean it. If they only have one horse, buy that one and give it to me," Fox said.

Berserker frowned at him, and Aquilla smirked.

"What? I'm the prettiest of the three of us, so if anyone should survive, it should be me. Aquillo, you find some clothes. We all stink, and we are all dirty, I refuse to continue this way when we have money."

"And what will you do, pretty boy?" Berserker asked.

"I will find lodging." Fox clapped twice. "Move it! Meet here at dusk."

THERE WEREN'T MANY shops in town. Aquilla passed a bread and spice store before she found the clothing and shoe store. She walked into a small store and grimaced. She was sure she could find something for her and Fox, but Berserker was another story. His colossal frame wouldn't fit neatly into any of the clothes that were already made, and that selection was small to begin with.

"Can I help ye, sir?"

Aquilla turned and saw a small woman with a long nose and sunken eyes appear from behind a curtain.

"Yes, ma'am. My friends and I need new clothes and shoes. We came across some trouble and had to leave our things behind."

"Hmm, and what size ye be needing, sir?"

"Call me Aquillo, please. Sir is my father. Two pairs each, so six sets all together. My first friend needs clothes about two sizes larger than me in height, but only one size in width. Mainly the arms and chest. My other friend is four sizes wider than me and two heads taller. Do you have anything?

"Hmm," she said again. "Ye sir, be no problem fitting ye smaller lads, but the big one…" she tsked and shook her head as if finding something for Berserker would be difficult if not impossible. The woman turned and walked back through the cloth that separated the shop from her inventory, Aquilla assumed.

When she returned, she held several pieces of clothes. "Mr. Fin be about the same size as yer friend. I made these for him, but he ain't picked them up yet. I'd be within my rights to sell them to you for a good price."

Aquilla nodded. "Name your price and I will pay it."

The woman looked Aquilla up and down. Aquilla realized the way she looked. Walking all day left sweat stains under her arms and down her back. A musty smell wafted from her. She moved from one foot to the other, uncomfortable under the woman's judging stare. Instead of waiting for the shopkeeper's judgment, she dug into her pocket and pulled out a gold coin.

"See, I can pay."

The woman's eyes widened. Aquilla could almost see the greed in them. She'd pay more for the clothes than normal, but she wouldn't be taken for a full fool either.

"I won't be asking where ye got the coin, but I will do business with ye. Come, let's get ye settled."

AQUILLA FINISHED HER purchases and met Fox and Berserker in the town center. Fox led them to the inn where he told them they could sleep and eat for the night. Once they arrived, Berserker left the horses with a boy, probably the same age as she was with specific instructions of care. When they walked inside, the innkeeper greeted them with smiles even though they all looked awful.

Fox walked them up the stairs and pointed to three rooms, all next to each other. Aquilla gave a silent thanks that she have her own room. Bathing would be difficult without her own room. She purchased more fabric to wrap around her chest. If she could, she'd burn the cloth that bound her now. It smelled terrible. Aquilla picked the third room of the three. Fox had the first room, and Berserker took the second. She stepped into her room and closed the door. Immediately she walked to the window and shut the curtains.

A knock sounded at the door. "Sir, I'm here with water for yer bath."

On her way to open the door, she spied the large wooden tub. Aquilla opened the door, and a young girl walked in, carrying two buckets of water in each hand. Aquilla reached to help her.

"No, sir, this be my job. I don't require yer helpin," she said.

Aquilla nodded and watched as she dumped the water into the tub.

"Just four more, and ye can bathe."

Aquilla nodded, and the girl left. She returned twice more than said her goodbyes and told her she'd return in an hour to take the dirty water out.

Excited to bathe, Aquilla didn't think to lock the door after the maid servant left. Without thinking, she stripped off her shirt and unbound her breasts. The door opened, and Berserker and Fox walked into her room. Aquilla turned around on instinct. Fox and Berserker stared. Aquilla pushed her arms to cover her breasts, cursing her stupidity. She looked into Fox and Berserker's face. They were both beat red and mumbling apologies as they backed out of the room.

"Mort! You were supposed to magic them," Aquilla yelled at her arm.

"What? What happened?" Mort asked.

"Forget it. It's all over now."

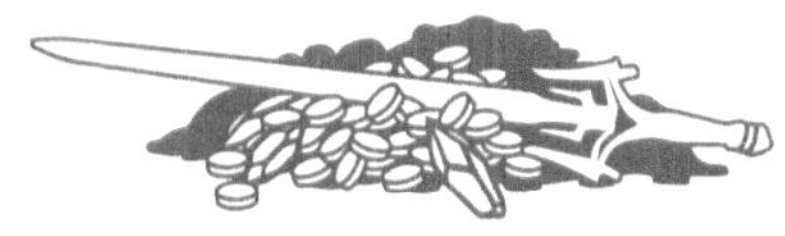

AQUILLA DRESSED. HER breasts were once again bound tightly. She'd pulled her hair into a perfect topknot. She was ready to face Fox and Berserker, along with all of their questions. She stood at the foot of the stairs, searching the sea of laughing men and women for Fox and Berserker. She found them sitting at a table in the corner near the fire. She gave them both a once over. It looked like their clothes fit. Berserker's arms were a little tight, but mostly his clothes fit. Fox's clothes fit him as if he had them tailor-made. Not too long, short, or tight fitting anywhere. The cream and blue colors of the fabric complemented his reddish orange hair and gold eyes.

Aquilla walked toward the corner and sat down across from Fox and to the side of Berserker. She braced herself. Berserker and Fox drank from their mugs, looking anywhere but at her. Aquilla sighed. If they weren't going to talk about it, fine, but she was hungry. She looked around for the server to order something, but this was her first time in an inn. She didn't know what to order. Earlier, she was smugly proud of herself for buying clothes for the first time.

Fox put his mug down and looked at her, then at Berserker, who was busy frowning at the fire.

"So, you're a woman. What's your real name then?"

She cleared her throat. "Aquilla."

"Not the most creative are you, Aquillo-I mean Aquilla," Fox said. Aquilla grinned.

"Why," Berserker said, then shook his head. "No, how did this come to be? I don't fight women, ever, but I did, and you won."

Aquilla looked at Berserker. He looked as if he would cry any moment. She tried to help him feel better.

"In your defense, I have trained my entire life, every day, with one of the best swordsmen ever known. I'd wager you can forgive yourself this once."

Berserker shook his head and turned back to glaring at the fire, whispering, "A female beat me. A small, delicate female."

Fox choked on his drink. "Berserker, I don't think Aquilla can be considered delicate by any man's measurement. No offense, Aquilla."

She shrugged. She desperately wanted to ask for help with ordering, but she was too shy to reveal she needed help with something so basic.

The server came to take Aquilla's order. She hoped whatever Fox ordered was good because she asked for whatever he was having. Berserker was still glowering at the fire, and Fox was looking at the other people in the inn. She had to deal with Berserker.

"Berserker, I know me being a woman comes as a shock to you, but before you found out that I'm a woman, we were working well together and on a critical mission. We promised the men that we would get their families to safety. At least help me with that then we can go our separate ways. Anyway, after we finish getting the families out, I have other business in the city."

"Does your other business have anything to do with the two guards who helped us earlier?" Fox asked.

"Yes, it does," she said.

He nodded back. "And you think to meet them alone?"

"If I have to," Aquilla answered and lifted her chin a bit.

Berserker joined the conversation. "How do you know they are friend or foe? I mean, they helped keep us in the cave where we were starved and beaten daily."

"My business with them has nothing to do with anyone else. I won't let them near the families, but I need them for something personal."

The server came back with their food, and any further talk was over. They shoveled the meat and mashed potatoes into their mouths, forgetting about anything but filling their empty stomachs.

CHAPTER THIRTY-THREE

It's Not You, It's Me

Garret looked in the mirror and adjusted his tie. He reached behind him for his jacket. King Daemon and his daughter would arrive at the gate in a handful of minutes. He'd forgotten about them in his excitement to have found Aquilla and a worthy match for his father. He would have to find someone to push Esmeralda off on for a while when he and Wulf went to meet Aquilla and her friends.

Garret had thought about Aquilla a lot over the last two years. He'd almost shifted and went looking for her, but he'd known better.

A knock sounded at his door.

"Come in."

Wulf entered his room. "Are you ready? They are nearly here."

Garret rolled his eyes. "Joy."

"At least act the part."

Garret turned toward Wulf, his hand in his pocket, rubbing his smooth marble. "Don't I always, Wulf? Today does not differ from any other day. I will play my part. Let's go."

AT THE GATE, KING DAEMON and his daughter Esmeralda's carriage waited. The King appeared first, turning back with his hand lifted to help his daughter out of the carriage. Garret saw her dainty foot covered in a pearl satin slipper first before glimpsing her shapely leg as she stepped out of the carriage. She was as beautiful as he'd heard. The sun glistened off her silky golden hair that fell perfectly down her back. Esmeralda had a perky nose, high, rosy cheekbones, and luscious lips. He had to admit that he paused a moment longer than necessary on her lips. He'd never say she was anything but beautiful on the outside. It was what lay within that was ugly. She coveted power, and she was willing to use her beauty as a tool to get it. While other dragons and men fell over themselves with the hope she'd acknowledge them, Garret stood aside. She wasn't what he was looking for.

Fierce hazel eyes set on a round face with a round nose, and a cute topknot popped into his mind. Garret smiled at the thought of Aquilla. Ever since he'd figured out who she was, she was all he could think about. How bold she was, how strong she was. How beautiful she was, inside and out.

He turned his attention back to the matter at hand. He couldn't greet Esmeralda while thinking of Aquilla. He wouldn't sully his thoughts of Aquilla by associating any part of her with Esmeralda.

Esmeralda walked toward his father and curtsied. His father grabbed her hand and kissed the back of it as any gentleman would.

"Another year has gone by, and you have grown more beautiful," his father said before reaching for Garret's hand. His father joined his hand with Esmeralda's. His father's intentions were obvious. He wanted to marry him off to Esmeralda, so through their marriage he would gain more land. Garret was a master at masking his emotions, so nothing but a smile appeared over his face as he held Esmeralda's hand. When, Esmeralda disgusted him. He loathed her touch and his father for forcing him. Seeing that his father already mentioned her beauty, there wasn't a reason for him to say it a second time. Instead, he bowed in respect and said, "I wish you a pleasant stay here, and I hope you find yourself in good company."

She smiled.

"Come King Daemon, let the kids get reacquainted while we talk in private. Garret, take good care of Esmeralda. Show her to her rooms and make sure she is settled."

Then his father and King Daemon resumed their walk toward the castle, leaving Esmeralda behind.

"So, we finally meet again, Garret."

"Prince Garret, Princess," he corrected.

She rolled her eyes, and he winked at her.

"What are titles between close friends?" she asked.

Garret smiled and wrapped her arm around her to escort her into the castle. "Even my good friends call me Prince."

Esmeralda scoffed. "Garret, I'll not call you Prince every time I need to say your name. We are more than close friends. You should treat me special because of it. Most men would be happy for me to remember their name much less insist on saying it."

Garret gave Esmeralda one of his signature grins. "It's not you. It's me. I'm not easily swayed by beauty, but if it means that much to you. Please, call me Garret."

"It doesn't mean that much, but I will call you Garret. What activities have you planned for us?"

Garret smiled. "I have much planned that I think you will enjoy. I will tell you once I have you settled in your rooms. Not even I am excused from following my father's requests."

Esmeralda nodded. "Very well."

GARRET CHANGED FROM his official clothing to the clothing he wore when he wanted to blend in. He'd left Esmeralda in the care of her servants. She was in her element, ordering them around and positioning her things. It didn't seem like she'd brought enough for two weeks. The amount seemed like she was planning on staying much longer. Garret filed that away to deal with at another time. He couldn't be everywhere at once. Right now, his priority was Aquilla.

While she was a great fighter, she still needed to learn how to kill a dragon, and Garret didn't know how he would sneak that into her training. He'd figure it out. He looked up at the sun. It was almost noon, and he would be late if he didn't leave right now. He walked out of his room and toward the servants' tunnels. Once he was outside, Wulf waited for him with a horse.

"Thanks," Garret said to Wulf.

"Cutting it close, aren't we?"

"I know, but Esmeralda was hard to get away from. I don't know how I will keep sneaking away. She's intent on attaching herself to me."

Garret mounted his horse.

"Wouldn't you be if you were her?" Wulf asked.

Garret grinned at Wulf and kicked his horse into a gallop. They couldn't be late.

CHAPTER THIRTY-FOUR

The Darkness That Found Me

Lilah returned to the cabin after another day at the market, trying to find out if anyone had seen or heard anything about her granddaughter. Her heart sank every time someone looked at her and told her no, but she had to keep up her story because she knew in her heart, Aquilla was out there somewhere.

The rumors of the lost warrior princess had traveled farther than Lilah had imagined. There were whispers everywhere. There were even a few secret groups forming to look for her so they could help her claim her throne. Lilah rubbed her forehead. Her skin felt tight. She hadn't shifted into her dragon form in too long, and she was becoming uncomfortable in her human skin, but she couldn't deal with that right now.

With all the whispers in every corner, it was only a matter of time before Athel would set out to find her himself. Lilah didn't know if that was a good or bad thing. She knew that hope of a different future was why everyone wanted to believe in her granddaughter, but what would happen if Athel found Aquilla and killed her? She was only a human. He could send his son or one of the other dragon warriors he had littered throughout his guard and army.

Lilah stopped pacing and sank onto Duncan's rocking chair. As she rocked, she thought about Aquilla. Before she knew it, sleep had taken her.

LILAH STOOD IN THE middle of a dark forest. She felt a chill run through her body; she knew this place. This was the place she tried to forget every day but remained a shadow in her mind.

"Lilah," she spun around, fearing the ominous creature with glowing eyes that haunted her dreams. Instead, a man appeared. He wore all white. His skin was alabaster, the opposite of the darkness that haunted her the last time she was here.

"You've changed," Lilah said.

"What you see on the outside does not always reflect the inside of a thing. An apple could look tasty and ripe for the picking, but once you bite into it, you find out it is rotten to its core. I think that sums me up, don't you?"

Lilah laughed. "A deceiver, absolutely."

The creature shook his head. "Aren't all dragons deceivers? We wear the clothing of humans to hide the beast within. When was the last time you shifted? When was the last time you spread your wings during the day to show your superiority over the foolish humans?"

"We don't do that anymore."

"Why!" the dark one yelled. "Why do we suppress what we are to please beings so inferior to us? We should rule over them. Show them through fire and claw that we, dragons, are the true and only predator they should fear and worship."

"Worship? I don't want to be worshiped by humans. I just want to be with my granddaughter."

"Your granddaughter is all you think of, but I know as well as you the only reason you cling so desperately to that child is to make up for the mistakes you made with her mother. Nothing, absolutely nothing, will absolve your feelings aside from you. You were the one who allowed your mate to say awful things to your daughter. You set back and said nothing."

"Stop it!" Lilah screamed.

He didn't. "She never knew how much you loved her because you did as your mate told you."

"I had to!"

"When your mate said don't talk to your daughter, you did it. When he disowned her, you did too. Face it, Lilah, you weren't strong enough. You still aren't strong enough. You can't even save your grand-daughter."

"I will save Aquilla no matter what."

"Will you?"

"Yes, you bastard," Lilah said.

"Good. Remember that feeling. I didn't call you here to discuss your granddaughter but to remind you of your end of the bargain. I feel the time is drawing near. You must be ready, but remember dear Lilah, what will happen if you neglect to finish your part of the bargain."

The creature's hand reached out and tilted her chin up. She looked directly into his glowing eyes. Lilah wrenched her chin from his grip and stepped back.

"I have forgotten nothing. How could I forget that I agreed to murder someone to save myself?"

"Oh dear Lilah, I can't help but see the darkness inside you, call it a part of the job."

"You are doing something to me. You're making me dark."

"Your actions belong to you, not me." The creature tsked. "I called you here to remind you of our agreement. I've done so. Now you can go."

Lilah woke. She wiped the sweat from her forehead and neck. She pulled her legs up, buried her face, and cried.

CHAPTER THIRTY-FIVE

One Of A Kind

Riding a horse wasn't as hard as Aquilla thought it would be. Mounting was difficult, but Fox helped her each time without asking questions. The last time they stopped, she mounted by herself.

They rode fast and entered the city with little time to spare. Berserker found a place to store their horses. He said it would be better to travel the rest of the way on foot. Aquilla didn't have an opinion because she'd never been out of the forest. She depended on her friends to help figure out the next steps.

Entering the capital city overwhelmed her senses. The capital was nothing like the small town they'd stopped at earlier. Everything here was brighter, louder, more smells both good and bad, and far more shops and tents selling everything from meat to swords and small pieces of jewelry.

She wanted to stop at several tents, but they were already cutting it close to the time they were supposed to meet Garreth and Wulf. Berserker and Fox hurried. Aquilla struggled not to fall behind. Sometimes people walked between them, separating her from them. More than once, she had to move out of the way for one of the elaborate carriages. Aquilla did not like how careless the drivers were about the people who walked in front of them. She wondered how many people were hurt because of these carriages that moved through narrow streets.

What Aquilla disliked the most was the clothing the women wore. Their clothes showed so much of their breasts. Aquilla couldn't imagine. She'd spent her entire life keeping her breasts bound and out of the way. She didn't see a reason for them at all. But these women used them as weapons to attract attention, and it worked. Aquilla watched a man nearly fall into the path of a carriage, because he worried more about watching a pretty woman than his own safety.

Aquilla stopped when she saw a man pull a woman into his shop. She tensed, ready to act, ready to protect. She took one step toward the shop, but a hand on her shoulder pulled her back. Aquilla followed the hand to Berserker's face.

"That's just his desperation. He means her no harm."

She watched the man and woman. She watched the man push item after item into the woman's face, begging her to buy something from him.

"Why is he so desperate?" Aquilla asked.

"I don't know, but I think it is worth finding out. There's a lot of things happening I've never seen before. You can almost taste the almost frantic desperation of the shop owners. It wasn't always like this."

Aquilla nodded. Fox came to stand on her other side and watched, shaking his head.

"I'll find out what is happening later. Look ahead. There's the spot we are to meet the guards. What if they are setting up a trap?" Berserker asked.

She didn't think there was a trap, but to be sure she'd ask Mort.

"Mort, can you sense anything wrong? Like a trap or something?" Aquilla waited. "Mort, are you okay?"

"I'm fine. I was sleeping. Do you pop up right away when you first wake up?" Mort asked obviously irritated.

"It's noon. Why are you just waking?"

"Maybe because I spent the night watching your back? Just because I'm not talking to you doesn't mean I'm not watching, cousin. Anyway,

I don't sense anything wrong. The guards are there waiting, but nothing seems out of place. Anything else?"

Aquilla smiled. "No, and thank you and not just for this but also for watching my back. You're like a silent sentinel."

Mort snorted and pulled from her mind once more.

When she came back to herself, she heard Berserker asking her what she thought about his plan. She hadn't listened to any of it.

"There isn't a trap, but they are already waiting. Let's go." Aquilla didn't wait for them to follow; she walked forward.

CHAPTER THIRTY-SIX

Dropped my fan

Garret shifted from foot to foot, upset that he picked a place so open to meet the group of three. He tried to avoid looking directly at anyone. Still, women kept circling him. Wulf thought him being uncomfortable was funny. Garret glared at him, which only made Wulf's smile widen.

Someone bumped into Garret from behind, again. "I'm sorry, I dropped my fan, can you please help me find it?"

Garret looked down and picked up the third dropped fan in fifteen minutes. He gave the woman the fan and went back to looking for Aquilla. When he felt the woman's hand touch his arm, he tensed. Garret didn't like when strangers touched him. His jaw clenched, and he pulled his arm from under her hand.

"Sir, would you enjoy some tea with me? It's the least I could do considering how you saved my fan."

"No, thank you," he said, still not looking at her. Finally, the woman left. Garret's eyes rolled.

"This is getting out of hand," Garret said.

Wulf smiled. "It is your own fault for being so handsome."

"Don't you start, Wulf."

He laughed.

Garret straightened. There she was, striding toward him, confident and dressed in men's clothing. He smiled. She walked straight up to him and stood in front of him. Her shoulders pulled back, and chin lifted.

He smiled down at her, and she didn't need to drop a fan or accidentally bump into him to be on the receiving end of it. It was her presence that made him smile. Her strength and leadership. Her fierceness. His dragon stirred.

"You made it," Garret said.

"We did. Although, Berserker thought it might be a trap."

Garret lifted a brow. "You didn't?"

"No, so what's next?" she asked.

"I know a place where we can eat and discuss our next steps. They have safe lodging there. I'll make sure you all have rooms. I know the owner." Garret smirked. He was the owner.

Aquilla looked behind her to the two men. They both shrugged. She turned back toward him. "Lead on, Garreth."

Garret looked back toward Wulf, who mouthed, "Garreth?" his eyes laughed with amusement. He couldn't think of anything else at the moment. Aquilla was no better at creating fake names either. They had that in common.

AS THEY WALKED, FOX inched closer to him. Garret noticed but allowed him to get closer because he had a few questions for Fox.

"What are you?" Garret asked.

From the corner of his eyes, he saw Fox's toothy smile.

"I suppose it is only fair that you should know what I am if I know what you are, but I'd advise you not to repeat it, especially not to Aquillo."

Garret corrected him. "Don't you mean Aquilla?"

"Ah, so you figured it out, hatchling prince. Good for you."

Garret and his dragon bristled. "This hatchling is stronger than you think."

"Are you stronger than a seven tail Kitsune?"

Garret's brows furrowed. "If you are a Kitsune, then why were you trapped in the cave for so long? You could have escaped with Aquilla and saved her from all of this." Garret asked, turning to face Fox.

"I could have, but Aquilla needed something from there. Speaking of Aquilla, you should know she is very special to me. I would be very put out if she was hurt, and if she's hurt, I won't stand down Little Dragon. Trust me. You won't like it."

"I'm not an easy enemy, Fox."

"Is that so? And I take it that is why you have a human girl fighting your father instead of you."

"It isn't a matter of if I can beat him. It is how I beat him that matters. I can't divide the kingdom. I can't be the one to do it."

"So, you have a helpless girl do it for you?"

Garret's jaw clenched. He couldn't say anything. He couldn't deny what he was trying to do—guilt rode him harder than the disguised threats from Fox.

"Nothing will happen to her. I promise you that," Garret said.

"Make sure of it, Little Dragon, make sure of it."

CHAPTER THIRTY-SEVEN

I'm The Best

Garret walked into the inn and straight to the back. He turned to make sure everyone was still behind him. He would have been happy if Fox somehow got himself lost, but he was there, right behind Aquilla. Garret found his table and pointed to it.

"Please, have a sit. I'll be right back. I need to get a server," he said to the group. His eyes landed on Aquilla as he walked past her. Not once had she looked at him to seduce, only in challenge. That was a first, which only made him smile. He navigated the tables and servers until he was leaning over the bar.

"Patrick, how are you?" Garret yelled.

"What brings you here, sir?"

"I'm with guests. We are sitting at my table. Send Beatrice to serve us. My friends will also need three rooms for a while."

"Yes, sir. I will get the rooms ready." Patrick nodded and left. Garret assumed he went to find Beatrice.

Garret returned to the table catching the tail end of Aquilla's plan for the families. She had a loose plan. She wanted to put the families on a boat and get them out of the city in two days time. Wulf asked how they would get the families to believe they should pack up everything and move on their word alone. Everyone was silent in thought after that.

"We just have to try. We can tell them everything we know about their husbands and hope they believe," Aquilla said.

Garret piped up. "I can pay for passage for them if that would help."

Aquilla gave him a curious look. Fox's eyes danced with mischief. No doubt he wondered how he was going to talk his way out of this.

"Use the coins you gave me. I don't need it. Wulf doesn't either. Neither of us have families to support."

Aquilla nodded. "Thank you, Garreth, but I don't think you should talk for Wulf. He may need the money."

Garret looked at Wulf, who grinned. His eyes shone with amusement.

"I agree with Garreth. Take my coins too," Wulf said.

"Thank you both. We have a plan now. We need to execute it with haste," Aquilla said, and all agreed.

BEATRICE REACHED OVER his shoulder to take his empty plate. Garret looked away as her breasts nearly rubbed against his face. He heard a grunt from across the table and saw Aquilla smiling at him and gesturing for him to take Beatrice up on her offer. Garret rolled his eyes and shifted away.

He shook his head. "Trust me, Aquillo, I don't want her attention."

Her face lost its amusement and settled back into business. Garret mourned the loss of her smile. "Tell me how I enter the tourney," she said.

"I already took care of that for you. I found a sponsor for you. He agreed to pay for your entry fees and armor. There's another little matter of swordplay we need to discuss."

"What about it?" she asked.

"I haven't seen how you handle a sword yet. One competition is sword fighting. Another is archery, then hand-to-hand combat. Are you okay with that?"

Aquilla turned her head to the side in thought. "The archery will be an issue. My father never taught me archery."

Garret nodded. "I can teach you that. You just need to be decent. I'm sure you will have good marks with everything else to make it to the top."

Aquilla smiled a genuine smile. His heart and stomach flipped over. "I'm not a decent anything. I'm the best and the strongest, period. You teach me how to use a bow and arrow, and I will hit the mark every time."

Garret smiled back. "I'll believe it when I see it," he said, shocked to find himself flirting with her. Her that he was supposed to think was a him. Garret cleared his throat. "I know a place where we can practice with no one watching. Walk straight two miles, turn left at the red house, and keep walking until you see a brown hall. Meet me there tomorrow, two hours past noon."

Aquilla nodded and stood. "Got it. See you tomorrow. I need to find Fox and Berserker. Thank you, Garreth, for everything."

Garret waved her off and watched her walk away.

GARRET MET WULF AT the entrance of the inn.

"Are they all settled?" Garret asked.

"Yes, but I think Fox and Berserker know that Aquilla is a woman."

Garret stopped. Anger coursed through him.

"There's no way I'm letting her stay there. One female with two men. No, not happening."

Wulf stood in front of Garret.

"What are you doing?" Garret asked.

"I'm standing in your way. Let her be. She can take care of herself, and I don't think anyone is encroaching on your territory."

"What are you talking about, Wulf?"

Wulf only smiled.

"What are you smiling about?" Garret asked annoyed.

"Nothing, nothing. I think this will be great entertainment for me. These old eyes haven't seen this in some time."

"What do you mean you haven't seen this?" Garret reluctantly turned around. He had to get back without a fighting woman in tow. He already had one of those waiting at the castle.

"Let it go, Little Dragon."

"Don't start," Garret said.

CHAPTER THIRTY-EIGHT

Witchy Nature

Garret and Wulf took the back way into the castle. Garret moved quickly to his room to dress in his princely clothing. He knew Esmerelda would soon look for him, and he needed to be wherever she expected to avoid her telling his father he hadn't been in the castle.

He'd just finished pulling on his waistcoat when someone knocked on the door.

"Prince Garret. Princess Esmerelda would like you to attend her."

He clenched his jaw. She'd summoned him, and that irritated him. Garret dropped his marble into his pocket and switched his personalities again. He was no longer a guard working to redeem himself. Now he was an aloof prince who was playing hard to get with a beautiful princess his father obviously intended for him to wed.

Garret sighed and wondered if he even remembered who he really was after all these years of pretending. He suspected he didn't.

GARRET KNOCKED ON ESMERALDA'S door. The door opened and Esmeralda flung herself onto him. Her soft floral scent and body pushed up against him. He backed away, and she pouted prettily.

"Garret, I'm dreadfully bored."

"What do you want to do?" he asked.

"Give me a tour of the castle. My father and I never needed to visit King Asthmoth."

"I can do that. Where would you like to start?"

"Outside."

Garret held his arm out for her. She wrapped her arm around his and settled close. Even though Esmeralda was beautiful and born to be a queen, he knew she wanted to be empress. It was her nature. Garret wanted a woman who was strong, kind, loyal, a good co-leader to his people, independent, dragon, and fierce. Aquilla was all of those things, except she wasn't a dragon. Garret pushed away silly notions of romance. Now was not the time to entertain those. He was about to overthrow an empire. He had to prioritize.

GARRET WALKED AROUND a corner following behind Esmeralda and found his father and King Daemon sitting outside talking about something cruel, Garret thought.

"Father," Esmeralda walked to kiss his forehead. Her father's hand reached up and patted his daughter's cheek.

"What are you doing outside?" King Daemon asked.

"Garret is taking me for a tour around the castle," she said, smiling as if the tour meant more than what it did. Garret barely stopped his eyes from rolling.

Not to be outdone in any aspect, Garret's father motioned him over. "Son, come sit down."

Garret sat down and picked up a small powdered pastry and popped it into his mouth. He had to appear relaxed. He was just a prince on a stroll with a pretty princess—no need to pay any attention to him.

"I was just telling King Daemon the troubles of running an Empire."

Garret thought it was more likely he was rubbing his empire in King Daemon's face.

His father picked up his goblet and drank deeply. He set it down and smiled. Must be wine. Day drinking was one of his father's vices. It had the unfortunate side effect of making him crueler than he was when he was sober.

"Where was I? Oh, we were talking about the rumors of a lost warrior princess circulating the empire. I put Alistair and his witchy nature on it. I'm sure he will find the person who started the rumor and snuff them out, just like that." For good measure, Garret's father snapped his fingers, signaling the death of a person he'd never met.

"I'm sure Alistair will root out your enemy, Father."

"Yes, it's what he is good at," his father agreed.

"What is the name of this lost warrior princess?" Esmeralda asked, sitting next to her father.

His father tapped a finger against his lip in thought. "It started with an A. I've already forgotten, Daemon, I just told it to you, do you remember?"

"Yes, we talked about how many ways we could torture her once we caught her at length; it was Aquilla."

"Yes, that's the wenches name!"

Garret's heart stopped, and he nearly fell out of his chair. Quickly, he pulled himself together.

"Enough talk about kingdom business. You two kids continue your walk. Be sure to take good care of Esmeralda, Garret," his father said. The gleam in his eye said it wasn't a request.

Garret stood and walked toward Esmeralda. He held his hand out for her to take, and he led her away. His mind reeled from what he just heard. It had to be a coincidence. Had to be.

CHAPTER THIRTY-NINE

Tidmarc heard from Astor who heard from Guvner

Lilah made her way to the city once more. She noticed the new merchants that set up. As she passed them, they all made promises that their wares were from exotic places unseen. Lilah kept walking, dazed. She was uncomfortable in her skin and heartsick. She wanted her granddaughter. She wanted to talk to her for the first time and hold her in her arms.

What color are her eyes? Would they be like her daughter's or Duncan's?

"Ma'am, over here."

Lilah turned her head and walked toward the tomato stand.

"I told ye, I would keep an ear out for news about the Princess, and I did. I be opening my store this morning, and one of the other merchants, Tidmarc, was telling me he heard from Astor who heard from Guvner that the princess was staying at mean ol' Patrick's inn. I told him to keeps it quiet. The Emperor would kill her if he found her."

Lilah grabbed the woman's arm. The rest of what she said was of no consequence. Aquilla was here. She had to find her. "Where is Patrick's inn?"

"Go straight down to the left for about a mile; it's the biggest inn on that block of shops. Ye really can't miss it. Be careful, ma'am. I hope for all of our sakes ye princess will take the throne back."

Lilah ran, careful to control her speed in front of the humans. Her heart soared. Joy and pride overwhelmed her. She made it. She was still alive. Finally, finally, she would see her granddaughter. Her last living legacy. Her reason to live.

LILAH WALKED INTO THE inn and sat in the corner. She'd wait there all day if she had to, just to see if Aquilla was here.

"What do ye have this morning?" a server asked.

"Biscuits, please," Lilah said as she settled into her seat to wait. Lilah watched and listened. She noticed three men walking down the stairs. She couldn't see the third man well, the two men were blocking him from her view, but she couldn't take her eyes off the group until she saw the third man.

"Shut up and do your jobs. We will meet back here one hour past noon. I have a place I need to be."

"You aren't going anywhere without me, Aquilla," a handsome man with striking golden-red hair said.

"And me," a tall brute of a man said.

The two men parted at the bottom of the stairs, revealing her granddaughter. She knew it was Aquilla the moment her eyes landed on her. She was beautiful. Her eyes, she'd finally seen her eyes—hazel like her mother's. Lilah stood. She would introduce herself and tell her everything she knew about her life and take her back to the cabin where she was safe, and they could plan together what to do about Athel. Her granddaughter was in front of her, only seven steps away. She took one step toward her but wobbled on her feet. She reached out and placed her hand on a table to hold her up. She watched as Aquilla walked away from her. Lilah's head spun and her heart raced. She took two more steps toward her before a blinding pain reverberated through her mind. A murderous intent came over her. She felt its presence before it spoke.

"You've found her. Well done. Now kill her."

Lilah shook her head. "My granddaughter? You want me to kill my granddaughter? I won't. I can't."

"You will, or I will do it for you. Either way, she dies. That was the deal."

"You knew all along. You tricked me!"

Lilah grabbed her head and pulled her hair. She fought the desire to shift to her dragon and push her claws into her granddaughter. A silent sob tore from her. She heard the murmurs from the people around her. They thought she was sick. She was more than sick, but there wasn't a doctor alive that could help her. Haltingly, she walked out of the inn. She could still see Aquilla in front of her.

The creature's voice echoed in her mind. "Kill her. Kill her. We made a deal."

Lilah grabbed her hair, pulling out clumps as she ran out of the inn in the opposite direction of Aquilla, careless of the humans and her speed. All she knew was she had to put distance between her and Aquilla. Dark laughter rang through her mind.

"Run away, Lilah, but you can't run away from me. I'm already a part of you, and I will take all of you if you refuse me. That is the deal."

"No, don't hurt her!" Lilah yelled.

"You broke our deal, so now it's my turn."

Lilah almost made it to the cabin before she felt the darkness covering her. Her soul shifted and changed, warping into something unnatural. She tried to fight it, she wanted to stop it, but she couldn't. She clung to the small amount of light left inside her, but it wasn't enough to overcome the darkness.

"Stop it. You're killing me. You're killing me," Lilah screamed.

"No, sweet Lilah, I'm possessing you."

Lilah's last thought, her last plea, was for Aquilla to run. Tears ran down her face, over her cheeks, and hung on her chin. Before her tears hit the ground, Lilah was no longer.

CHAPTER FORTY

Pretty Boy's Pride

The next morning, Aquilla, Berserker, and Fox met in Fox's room after breakfast.

"I know a guy who could help with safe passage. The question is, how many people are we talking about?" Berserker asked.

"According to the names the men gave us, we need five seats on a ship to Darka's port in the north and four to Pushki's port in the south," Fox said.

"We need them on a ship tomorrow," Aquilla said.

"I will see it done," Berserker said confidently.

"Take Garreth's and Wulf's coins with you. If you need more, we will pay. We have to get them out. While you are at the docks. Fox and I will visit the three families and try to convince them to pack and leave tomorrow."

"How will they know which ship to get on?" Fox asked.

"A code. We can give them a code," Aquilla said.

Berserker nodded. "How about we just give them the name of the ship? Tell them to find his ship, The Great Lady. I will make sure the captain will have someone there to direct them to where they need to go. The families going north will use one code and the families going south another. Depending on the code, the captain's man will take them to the right ship. It's the best we can do on so little time."

"Good plan. Let's get to work. We don't have much time," Aquilla said. Looking at the position of the sun, the day was burning quickly, and she still had to meet Garreth at two hours past noon.

IT TOOK LONGER THAN Aquilla thought it would to convince the three families that they should leave, but they did it. At least the families said they would go. She hoped for their sake that they would. She even gave them money just in case meeting up with their spouses became difficult. She did her best. She did everything she could to help those from the cave. Now, she had to set her sights on an entirely different enemy that would require far more than a few conversations and the handing of coin here and there. It was time to bring down an empire.

"He said a red house? I don't think it gets any redder than this, Aquilla," Berserker said, gesturing to the two-story bright red house on the corner.

"He told me to turn left here."

The group turned left and walked past two small hut houses when they saw the hall. They walked to the door and knocked. No one answered, so they walked inside. The place was large and empty.

Fox peaked his head into several rooms.

"Nothing in the rooms. I think we are alone."

Aquilla's eyes found a wall filled with swords. There were long swords, short swords, and swords that curved, which she'd never seen before. Then there were staffs. She and her father used staffs often when they practiced. She lifted a hand to touch one, memories flooded her, threatening to break the dam that held back her grief.

"You made it! And you found the swords." Garreth said as he walked into the hall.

"I appreciate a good sword. I once dreamed of having the best sword ever made and fighting in a glorious battle with it."

Berserker stood next to her and whispered. "I'm concerned about your childhood. Doesn't seem like there was enough lessons on being a lady."

Aquilla gave Berserker a *you think* look and shoved her elbow into his side.

Garreth stopped in front of her. "Alright, Aquillo, are you ready to spar?"

"Always," she answered.

Garreth turned around and nodded to Wulf, who whispered something to Berserker and Fox. They both nodded and walked into a room with Wulf. Aquilla turned toward Garreth.

"Where is he taking my friends?"

"Unfortunately, nobody can witness me fight."

"But, aren't I?"

"Yes, but that is different. I promise no harm will come to them."

"What kind of guard are you? Who cares if you can't fight. You watched plenty of others fight at the caves. I'm sure you watched Berserker fight, but now, because you are afraid you don't want him to watch you? I think that's childish."

Garreth smiled at her, and her stomach did a flip.

"I never said I was afraid. I just like to keep some things to myself; it gives me the upper hand in a fight. You never know who will become your enemy one day."

Aquilla couldn't argue that, but still, she didn't like not seeing her friends.

Garreth ignored her discomfort. "What type of sword would you like?"

"Long sword."

"Good choice," Garret said and threw the sword to her. She snatched it from the air. Garreth picked up a long sword of his own and circled her. She took her stance.

"Your stance is good," he said.

Annoyed that he was complementing her, she demanded that they get on with it. The atmosphere changed from conversation to determination. Excitement ran along her spine, trailed by adrenaline. Aquilla loved a good fight. She moved her sword and stance from a middle stance to a back right. She pointed her sword down on her right and held it for a moment before she charged. Aquilla swung her sword up and brought it down. Garreth stepped back, blocking her strike, but she'd just begun. She moved in again. Her sword repositioned to her middle stance. Then she moved, striking him again and again. Aquilla felt the familiar vibrations run up her arms as her sword clashed with Garreth's. She knew, soon, the pain would subside, and nothing but the fight would matter. Not Garreth, not her secrets or his, nothing but the pureness of the dance between swords.

Garreth went on the offense, and she blocked strike after strike. He was faster than her father, but she was in the zone. Nothing would get through when she was in the zone. Garreth spun with his sword wrapped around him in defense. She went low, and he flipped back, coming up into a fighting stance. Aquilla didn't hesitate. She went after him again, her mind at peace, looking for the opening. Looking for his weak spot. He'd protect this spot. It wasn't his heart, but she'd figure it out. Instinctively, everyone defended their weakest point.

There, she found it. She was graceful when she spun around Garreth, her sword moving around her waist and back as she went. Aquilla stopped behind Garreth and pointed her sword, directly against his spine.

Garreth stiffened and dropped his sword.

"Aquillo. I'm unarmed," Garreth said. It took longer than it should have for her to pull back.

She moved away and walked toward the wall and hung the sword. When she turned to the right, she saw Fox and Berserker staring at her open-mouthed with an angry Wulf standing behind them. She supposed they didn't like being separated either. She smiled, happy to see her friends safe. They didn't return her smile; they all kept staring at her. Then she looked at Garreth. He stared at her, as well.

"What? What is it? I told you I could fight," Aquilla said.

Did she do something wrong? Her father told her that sometimes when she zoned out, she became too strong. He cautioned and encouraged her to try to obtain that zone when she was practicing, but not when she was sparring. Oh.

"I'm sorry, Garreth. My father told me I shouldn't zone out like that when I was sparring, and I forgot. I didn't mean to hurt you if I did. Are you okay?"

Garret nodded, then swallowed. "I think the sponsor will be happy with your skill. It certainly outclasses mine, and that is very difficult to do."

Aquilla knew she'd done something wrong. Garreth seemed mad, and the others were still staring at her.

"I don't just zone out like that for anyone if that helps. I have to consider you a worthy opponent; otherwise, it's unfair, which is dishonorable."

That sounded a lot better in her mind, but once she said it out loud, she regretted it immediately. She took a different approach because if the pretty boy's pride was pricked, she didn't have the time to console him.

"What's next? I proved myself to you as you requested."

"That you did and more. Come here every day to practice with me. We will get your armor, sword, and whatever else you need. Aquillo, you are more than I could ever have asked for. Our plan will work. I can feel it."

She was happy with his declaration, and she could use the extra practice. It had been a while.

AS THEY WALKED BACK to the inn, Aquilla realized she had nothing left to do for the afternoon. Fox and Berserker's long legs made their strides long. It took some fast walking and sometimes jogging to keep up with them, but when they reached the inn, she'd grab some coins and ditch her friends to explore the city alone for the rest of the day at her speed.

CHAPTER FORTY-ONE

Let Me Be Clear

Garret and Wulf sped back to the castle. Garret's mind raced as he tried to connect the dots of the mystery that was Aquilla.

"So, are we going to talk about what happened?" Wulf asked.

"Humans can't move like that. Wulf, I need all the information we have on the Asthmoth line. Can you get that for me?"

"Yes."

Garret's mind flipped back and forth between replaying the fight between him and Aquilla and the warrior princess story his father told him. What had he stumbled upon, and how would that change things? Garret shook his head. One step at a time. First, he needed to confirm her identity; then he would think about the next steps, but now he had Esmerelda to deal with.

EVER A DUTIFUL SON, Garret stood in front of Esmeralda's door. He couldn't draw his father's attention by disobeying him. He lifted his hand and knocked. He heard movement behind the door before it opened.

"Garret, hello, what brings you to my door today?"

"I was wondering if you wanted to go to the market with me? I could show you around, and we could stop at the arena."

"That sounds wonderful. Let me grab my lady's maid and fan."

"I will meet you at the stables."

GARRET AND ESMERALDA walked through the market. She pulled him into a dozen stores. Garret pretended to listen to her all the while he replayed the fight between him and Aquilla. The spot where she aimed her sword was the only way to kill a dragon. How would she have known?

"Look at this, Garret!" Esmeralda exclaimed. Garret moved in closer to see what terrible thing she found this time. "Isn't this color beautiful? I haven't seen the like anywhere. What is it called?"

Garret hated the color and all the outrageous colors the noble wore. He stuck to the basic colors of his family crest a deep red, white, silver, and gold. Everything he owned was a variation of those colors.

"I believe that color is called yellow," Garret said.

"It is magnificent. It's vibrant and yells look at me. I want a dress made from it. Maybe I could have it made in time to wear to the tourney."

Garret didn't care. "Maybe. Would you like me to purchase that for you? As a gift from one friend to another?"

She grinned at him. "Silly boy, of course, you will purchase this for me. In the future, you'll be responsible for all of my purchases. You might as well have some practice."

The pasted-on smile he wore slipped just a little. He wouldn't be tied to her. She wasn't for him.

Esmeralda called to her lady's maid that traveled with them. "Frances, go fetch the shopkeeper. I want to buy an entire bolt of this color."

The middle-aged woman walked toward Esmeralda. "My lady, how can I assist you?"

Esmeralda's beautiful chin inched up. "Assist me? You have yet to provide any assistance. A noble couple comes into your store, and I had to fetch you for assistance. Shouldn't you have been beside me this entire time asking about my needs?"

The shopkeeper bowed. "Yes, my lady, I'm sorry."

This was one of his people, not hers. She wouldn't speak down to them. Garret stepped up and grabbed the shopkeeper's arms, pulling her up. "Please do not apologize. You have done nothing wrong. On the contrary, it seems that you have a lot of customers, and we all have to wait our turn. That's only fair. If you would be so kind as to package up a bolt of this and send the material to Lady Gwen's place to use for a dress for the young lady, I would appreciate it."

Once the shopkeeper left, Esmeralda whirled on him.

"How dare you speak over me? When I am handling servants or other womanly manners, it is not your place to pass judgment. It is mine. That is what the lady of the house does."

Garret grabbed her lightly by the elbow and walked toward the front of the small store to pay for the bolt of fabric. While he walked, he bent down to whisper to her. To anyone looking, they appeared like lovers sharing a secret, but the truth was he was done.

"You dare talk down to one of my people as an outsider? I won't have it. Let me be clear. My father's wants and mine aren't the same. He may want a marriage between us, but I do not, and if I had any doubts, after spending the day with you, I don't anymore. I listened

to how you talk and treat people disgusts me. Here's what is going to happen. You will go to my friend's shop, Clever Lady. You will be on your best behavior or by the dragon gods, I will take you to the dungeons and leave you there."

"You wouldn't. My father wouldn't allow it."

Garret smiled. "Don't you know? None alive can beat my dragon. Your father and mine included. I choose not to wield my strength, but that doesn't mean I have none. I have enough power to do whatever I want and not worry the least about the consequences. My people, their safety, and my care for them is what controls me, so I advise you to change your nasty attitude."

Garret straightened up and reached into his pocket. He sat a silver piece on the table and waved off the older lady when she tried to give him change. He also waved off Esmeralda. He left her to figure her way to Lady Gwen's shop, and by the time she was finished, he'd circle back to take her back to the castle but suffering her any longer was not an option. Garret wasn't worried that she'd tell his father what he said. Her pride was too great. She'd rather swallow nails than admit embarrassment.

Once Garret was out of the fabric shop, he turned the opposite direction of where Esmeralda needed to go.

He hadn't realized he was hungry until he smelled the fried cheese. He drifted toward the smell. His anger still held him tight in a fist. After all his people went through with his father, the last thing he was going to do was stand by and watch some power hungry female dragon mistreat them.

"How much for the cheese?" Garret asked the young boy.

The boy looked up and blew his black hair out of his eyes. "Two copper coins, sir."

Garret nodded. "Give me three pieces in that case."

The boy smiled. Although Garret's father never included him in the discussions of court, Garret knew he'd raised the taxes, and many of the merchants didn't bring home any money after they paid them. Maybe these rumors of a warrior princess were something necessary to keep hope alive for a better tomorrow. That day was coming quickly. He'd chosen the right person. She would win the competition and kill his father, ending his tyrannical rule.

Garret walked up the road, dodging a few puddles of tossed water over a horse's urine, which helped keep the smell down and walked into Marcus's shoe store.

CHAPTER FORTY-TWO

Half The Price

Aquilla stopped at a shoe store. She thought to buy Fox and Berserker some new boots. An old man shuffled to her as she entered.

"Young sir, what can I do for you?"

Aquilla walked to him and instinctively helped to hold the old man up.

Where are his children? Why is he here alone?

"I'm looking for two pairs of your finest boots for my friends," she said.

"The finest will cost you, young sir."

"I will take care of the cost if you show me to the boots."

The old man took the arm Aquilla offered and pointed toward the open area that faced the market street.

"Sir, why are you here alone? Where are your children or helpers?" Aquilla asked, her words laced with genuine concern.

He ignored her. "Look here, young sir, these shoes are one of a kind, made of the best leather. Inside there's cotton to help keep your feet warm, but the stitching is perfect. Not a drop of water would make it inside this boot. The high boot is the new style, and I have them in several bright colors."

Aquilla smiled. He didn't want to answer her, but that she had to know. "Old man, you said they were one of a kind, then why do you have so many?"

He stuttered through an answer. "I mean, you won't find this boot anywhere else. Not made with this level of skill."

Aquilla nodded and looked at the wares. They seemed like good boots. In truth, she wouldn't know, but still she wanted her question answered.

"Ah, I see, but who is here to help you if another customer comes?"

The old man released her arm and frowned. "Why do you care, boy? Did you come to rob me? Take an old man's last coin? Take it. I don't care anymore. This emperor has already taken everything from me. He took my boys, and he's taking my livelihood. Go on. Take the money. When you do, do me the favor of killing me too. I don't know why I hang on anymore."

The old man laid down on the ground and closed his eyes. Aquilla didn't know if she should laugh or cry. He was being a little dramatic, but she hadn't missed the grief in his eyes.

"Old man, stop this and stand up. Come, let's sit down and rest awhile."

Aquilla pulled him up and looked around for a place to sit. She found a stool in front of the entrance. She set the old man down and crouched in front of him. "Are you hungry? I can get you something to eat."

He shook his head. "I'm just tired."

Aquilla's heart broke. She stood and walked behind him. "Just sit there. I can help for a while."

Aquilla picked up shoes that fell from the table—setting to rights the boots that were misplaced.

"I thought you were going to rob me. Why are you cleaning?" the old man said.

"I was never going to rob you, old man."

The old man's cough turned into a wheeze. Aquilla walked toward him and gently patted him on the back.

"I'm fine. Get out if you're not going to rob me."

"But I'm helping you," Aquilla said.

"If you want to help, you can lower taxes."

"Is it really that bad? I'm not from here. I came for the tourney," Aquilla added as she didn't want him to ask her any more questions.

"Ah, you foolish young men are careless with your lives. My boys fought to try to keep this land from being taken by the Emperor. They died young, but they didn't want to. They wanted to live to get married, have some children, but now they will never get the chance, and here you are throwing your life away for some tyrant's enjoyment."

Aquilla bent over and picked up a bright green woman's boot and placed it on the table. "I don't know, old man. I might just win."

He scoffed. "That's no better! Then you become that fool's killer."

Aquilla didn't say anything. She kept cleaning. They sat in silence for a while. He sat and watched the people while Aquilla cleaned and set things to right.

"Boy, let me tell you something."

Aquilla walked toward him and stood off to the side, back turned against the door staring at the man's wrinkled face, gaunt eyes, and shaky hands.

"If you want to be a hero, you have to stand for something righteous. You have to stand for the people. It's easy to get caught up in wanting more for yourself. You want the nice boots and clothes so you can impress the pretty girls, but there's more to life than pretty girls and fancy clothes. Anyway, look at me; once I was like you. Ready to whip my sword out against any foe. I even worked my way up to the castle. I spent most of my life ignoring what was happening around me. I was busy with myself. I was busy proving myself to the rich so I could be accepted. I made myself talk like them, walk like them, even look like them. Then one day, I came across a man I knew beating a woman for stepping on his boot. His boot! I stopped him and helped the lady up. She wasn't noble. She was just a shopkeeper's daughter, but none of that mattered when I saw her beaten down in an alley for something so petty. I opened my eyes and ears. For the first time, I heard, and I didn't like what I was hearing. I saw things, and I didn't like what I seeing. I felt lost. I'd worked so hard to become one of them, but I would never be one of them. I was low born but good with a sword. Won many a tourney in my day, I even helped slay a dragon, made a name for myself, you see. Like you want to do. But none of that mattered after I realized what kind of selfish and petty people were around me. I went back to the shopkeeper's shop and asked about his daughter. She stood close to where you're standing now and thanked me for asking about her. I hadn't been thanked for many years. She thanked me for saving her from an injustice that should have never been. I couldn't go back. I did what you are doing now. I started helping around her father's shop. She started healing, and I noticed she was beautiful. She spoke terrible English, but I came to love it, I came to love her. I married her, you see, and bought this shop from her father. I took up the people's war against tyrants like this emperor, but it seems there's no one left to fight for the people. We will all lose if this doesn't end. If we don't die, our children will. We can't afford food. We can't afford coals for heat. We can't afford to keep our shops open. We will all lose if a hero doesn't rise."

Aquilla wanted to tell the man she was that hero. She would stop the tyrant, he just needed to hold on a little longer, but she couldn't. "Old man, stick around. Life may surprise you."

"I hear about this lost princess that has come to save us, but she'll need help. She can't do it alone."

Aquilla perked up. "What lost princess?"

"I don't know, but everyone swears by it. Some say they've even seen her."

"What's her name?"

"Aquilla, the lost warrior princess. I think she's a myth, someone who we invented to give us hope."

Aquilla's mouth opened and closed. How many women were named Aquilla in this city, and what were the chances of two Aquilla's running toward the same goal.

"I tell you what, old man. If this Aquilla exists, she has my sword."

"And mine too!"

Aquilla turned around, shocked to see Garreth leaning lazily against the wall behind her. How long had he been there? Was the old man blind? Why hadn't eh said anything about Garreth.

Garreth walked up to the man and squeezed his shoulders.

"Oh, here's a ladies man, boy. Don't get caught up with him. He's nothing but a ne'r do well."

Garreth laughed. "You say that every time I come here. Do you have my boots?"

"I sent your stupid boots to that hall. Don't come near me."

Garreth laughed again, and Aquilla watched as he began rubbing the old man's shoulders. "You speak of this lost princess. I think she's real. I think she will save us, and if I ever come across her, I would gladly watch her back."

"I bet you would you rake. Stop touching me," the old man said.

"But you are so tense. Have you rested as the doctor told you to?"

"I'm not listening to the doctor. I know how to die just fine, thank you, and I can do it for half the price."

Aquilla and Garreth laughed.

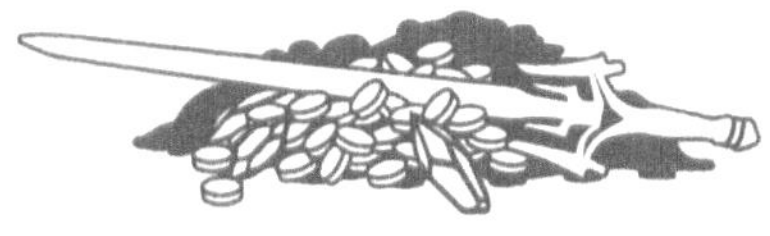

AQUILLA AND GARRET left the old man sitting in his chair, yelling for them not to come back. Aquilla was sure she would.

"What brings you to the market?" Garret asked.

"Exploring."

"What have you done so far?"

Aquilla shrugged. "The old man distracted me. I only went to one hut that sold fried cheese. Have you ever tasted it? It's very good."

Garret smiled down at her. "I had fried cheese before I went to the shoe store too. You have to taste the best buns ever made. Come with me." Before he could think better of it, he grabbed her hand and pulled her toward Lily's bakery. Together they ran through the bricked roads dodging horses and ladies, laughing as men cursed them for running.

"Here," Garret said, pulling Aquilla to a stop. They were both bent over, breathing hard. Garret, of course, was faking it, but still, he was having fun just like their time in the forest all those years ago.

"Come on. My treat," Garret said to a grinning Aquilla.

A beautiful woman appeared with long black hair that flowed down her back. Her dark green eyes reminded Garret of the forest trees. "Is that my handsome connoisseur?"

"I'm back for more of your delicious baked goods. I brought a friend with me this time."

Aquilla gave Lily a small smile.

"Another handsome boy for my collection."

Garret pulled Aquilla to him. "No, he's mine."

The shocked expression of Aquilla and Lilly made Garret smile. He managed to hold in a bark of laughter. Neither of them knew he knew Aquillo was really Aquilla. She struggled to pull her hand from his, but he held her to him. He liked the feel of her next to him. She was lethal in a fight, but there was still a piece of her that was all woman, and he noticed. Garret noticed her eyes, her pouty lips, and perfect cheek-bones. He wished he could see her hair down like Lily's. He wanted to run his fingers through her hair.

Reluctantly, Garret let Aquilla go and turned back to Lily. He winked at Lily, and she gave him a knowing smile before turning to pick out two buns. Garret paid her and pulled Aquilla outside to sit and eat with him.

"What should we do next?" Garret asked.

"I don't know. It's getting late. Maybe I should get back. I'm sure Fox and Berserker are worried. I didn't tell them I was leaving or where I was going."

Garret forgot he had to get back to Esmeralda.

"You're right. We should get going. See you tomorrow."

Aquilla stood and wiped her hands down her pants. "Be safe."

"You too," Garret answered.

CHAPTER FORTY-THREE

Enough Games

Once he and Esmeralda arrived back at the castle, she dismounted and never spoke a word to him. Garret wasn't upset. He spent the ride back to the castle, thinking about the day he spent with Aquilla. The way her hand felt in his and the look on her face when he claimed her as his. Her kindness to the shoe keeper. She was the total opposite of Esmeralda. She was exactly right.

Garret walked toward his wing of the castle on the far east side. As he walked, Wulf appeared as he usually did, stepping in stride with him.

"My Prince, we need to talk urgently."

"Okay, we can talk in my rooms."

They walked up the spiral of stairs leading to Garret's rooms. Garret opened the door and let them in. He gestured to the table and chairs in his receiving room.

"So, tell me. What is it?" Garret asked before he sat down.

"I checked into the Asthmoth's line and found Lilah and Asthmoth had a daughter who married a human."

Garret nodded. He knew this.

"Before she was killed, there was a brief mention of her being pregnant with a half breed child. It was buried within the text, easy to overlook. I doubt Asthmoth even knew one of the archivists recorded it. He no doubt ordered the child out of the lineage with her heritage and all."

Garret did not know this. "Naturally, he would. What is a child that is half dragon and half human? I didn't even know the two could successfully mix."

"I don't think there's a record of it happening until now."

"Until Aquilla. Well, this explains a lot, doesn't it?" Garret asked.

Wulf nodded. "It explains why she was able to get out of the pit in the caves and why she could beat you and Berserker in a fight."

"If she's half dragon, does that mean she can shift?" Garret asked.

"I don't know. I don't know if she knows she's half dragon. If I had to guess by her manners and who her father was, I doubt he got around to telling her."

Garret sighed. "I'm both pleased and disheartened by this news. If she can shift, this will only aid her in a fight against my father, but if she really is the crown princess, once she topples my father, she will become queen, and I don't think Aquilla set out to do that. Unlike most women, I think if she found that out, she'd run."

Wulf nodded. "And I don't think that's the end of her secrets. You really know how to pick them, my Prince."

Fury and frustration erupted inside. "Enough games. If all of this is true, its time she knew, and it's time for her to come clean. I have had enough. We aren't playing a card game. People's lives are at stake. Her life is at stake. I won't let her go into this fight without knowing everything that might aid her in getting out of it alive. If that means telling her she's a princess and a dragon, then so be it. Come on. We need to talk to her tonight."

AQUILLA WALKED INTO the inn and knocked on Fox's door.

He swung it open and pulled her in. "Where have you been?"

"I was out looking around."

"Without your handsome escort?" Fox teased, which made her happy. They were both talking again and laughing with each other. "Did you meet someone while you were out or maybe you kissed a boy? I must say, your father would not approve, so on behalf of him, I would need to thrash the boy," Fox said.

"Of course not. How would that look two boys kissing?" Aquilla shook her head and bit into the chicken leg, juice dripped down her chin. She wiped it off with her sleeve. Fox grimaced.

"Aquilla, you realize you really are a girl, right?"

"Obviously," she said.

"But girls don't—" Fox was interrupted by the door opening. Berserker barged in.

"She's back? I heard her voice. Aquilla, where have you been?"

The chicken leg hung from her mouth as she looked between Fox and Berserker. Slowly she chewed as they watched her. When she finished, her hands were covered with the chicken grease. She wiped them down her dark pants. Fox shook his head as if he were wounded.

"What is wrong with you two?" Aquilla asked.

Berserker closed the door and walked into the room. He sat on Fox's bed to Fox's great annoyance. "You were gone, and neither of us knew where you went. I didn't know if you were kidnapped and killed...or worse. You can't just walk off by yourself. There are rules for women."

"Do I look like a woman who follows those rules? Anyway, someone could *try* to kidnap me, but they wouldn't find me such easy prey this time around. I wasn't—I wasn't exactly in my right mind when I allowed myself to get kidnapped before," Aquilla said, remembering the pyre, the fire, the embers and ash that floated up into the dark skies.

Fox made a joke and they all laughed together, and they talked until night fell about nothing and everything. Berserker spoke about his mother and sister, who he intended to visit once they were finished here. Fox didn't have much to say about his past, and Aquilla found that strange, but she didn't mention much about her past either. They both listened and responded to Berserker, who had a nice story to tell. One that didn't end in tragedy, like hers, and maybe like Fox's too. Perhaps that's why he wasn't talking either. Aquilla stood, grateful for a moment of normal before everything changed.

CHAPTER FORTY-FOUR

Come Get Some

Aquilla lay in bed, not able to sleep. Thoughts of Garreth ran through her mind. She remembered the feel of his hand in hers. Both of their calloused hands pushed together. Even though she'd beat him earlier, he didn't hold it against her. He treated her with kindness as well as the old shopkeeper.

She tossed and turned several more times.

"What is it?" Mort asked.

"I can't sleep."

"I have an idea," Mort said.

"What?"

"We could go for a swim. There's water nearby, I can sense it."

Aquilla thought it over. A swim wouldn't be a bad idea. Especially if she could make Mort happy. He never asked for much. Aquilla sat up. "Let's go for a swim."

SHE RAN TOWARD THE docks. The largest body of water Mort could sense. She climbed down the hillside, half-walking, half-sliding. Her feet hit the ground, and she ran up the dock past the last boat to the very end.

"Mort, you still want to swim?"

"Yes!"

"What should I do?"

"Put your arm in the water," Mort said.

Aquilla pushed her arm into the water and felt Mort uncoil.

"Don't go too far, Mort."

Aquilla pulled her tunic and pants off, folded them on the edge of the pier, and dived into the water. She felt something smooth slither and glide under her body. She lay her hand on Mort's true form. He was long, not as long as his parents, but not far off. Mort swam around her, and she floated on her back, relaxed. She wished she could have taken off her underwear and the wrap around her breasts. The skies were dark and hiding the moon. She closed her eyes, not worried about being seen by anyone. She was far from the busy part of the dock, and only someone who could fly would see her from below. She was wrong. She should have worried.

AQUILLA'S EYES WERE closed, so she didn't see the two dragons land nearby, not that she'd ever imagined two dragons would be anywhere. They were supposed to be extinct, killed by her kind, but when she opened her eyes sensing something wasn't right, she saw a ball of fire hurtling toward her.

"By the gods, there are dragons. Mort! Get out of the way," she screamed from her mind to his. Aquilla dived underwater. Mort came to her. She straddled his back. He sprung out of the water, roaring his displeasure. She tried wrapping her arms around him so she wouldn't fall off, but her arms weren't long enough. Mort jumped straight into the air. He let out another fierce roar. Aquilla's body shivered with fear.

The dragon roared back and shot more fire at Mort. He deflected the fire and spit something green at the black dragon.

"Mort, I'm going to fall."

"No, you aren't. You are my rider. Just give me a minute."

"What are you even saying right now! I'm—I'm going to pass out."

"Pull it together, Aquilla, and fight."

"With what?"

"I don't know, think of something. I'm a little busy here."

"Why are you throwing up on the dragons, Mort? That's not helping either!"

"What are you talking about? That's acid."

"Oh, so that hurts them?"

"Aquilla, not now, we have to fight. You have to. There are two of them. I'm not old enough to handle two, and I can't beat them both."

And that did it. Nobody was going to take someone from her again. Never again. Aquilla closed her eyes and took a deep breath. She didn't know what she needed to do, but she knew the answer was somewhere inside her, she just needed to embrace it. She needed to remember. She needed to free it.

"Aquilla! He's behind me, I can't block it, and I won't get into the water quick enough. Help me."

"Come on, come on," she said to herself, and then time stopped. She stood on top of glowing iridescent water. Lolanthe stood in front of her. She reached up and stroked Aquilla's cheek. "You've suffered much Little One, but I'm here now. Give over to me and let me help you." Lolanthe held her arms out, and Aquilla walked into her embrace, wrapped her arms tightly around Lolanthe's waist. Her body warmed, bright light replaced Lolanthe, but she still felt her embrace. Aquilla had to close her eyes against the brightness. When she opened them, Lolanthe was gone, but she could still feel her comforting her, loving her.

Time sped up, and Aquilla was back in the thick of things with the dragons and Mort.

Aquilla jumped off Mort and shifted mid-air into a dragon. She saw her reflection in the water. She was enormous. The sound of her wings beating was loud against the silence of the night. She roared again, turning her attention toward the gold and black dragons.

Aquilla heard and saw everything, but the dragon, Lolanthe, was in control. She was a passenger sharing her pain, body, power with Lolanthe.

"You dare to attack someone under my protection?" Lolanthe roared. "You dare to come after me! I am the beginning and the end. I am the undoing and the making if you want a fight. Come get some."

Aquilla smiled. She couldn't have said it better.

They both watched as the dragons flew away.

"Did they run from us?" Aquilla asked.

"Looks like it, Little One."

Under normal circumstances, Aquilla would hate being called Little One, but with Lolanthe, it fit, and she liked it as much as she liked when her father used to call her his little Lilly.

Lolanthe flew to the woods and landed. "Here you go, little one."

And before she knew it, she was back to herself.

"Thank you," Aquilla said and raced back down to the water to find Mort.

"MORT," AQUILLA CALLED to the water's surface while she pulled on her tunic, pants, and boots. "Mort," she said with more urgency.

Then she saw the small snake wiggling toward her. She scooped him up, and he climbed up her arm. She breathed in relief.

"I don't think we will go swimming again for quite some time. That was crazy. Mort, you were fierce. I underestimated your ability. You are amazing and to think all that fits on my arm. And then me! Did you see me? I'm a dragon—a real life, white dragon, which is pretty amazing. I don't know. This is all insane. How did I become a dragon? Was it in the caves? I knew something happened to me in the caves."

Aquilla ran back to the city, following the same path she took to the docks, worried that the two dragons came into the city and hurt people. Hurt her friends. As she ran through the city, she didn't see any fire or smoke. Where had they gone?

"Should we warn the people that dragons are back?" Aquilla asked Mort.

"I'm going with no because self preservation. If people went dragon hunting, they would hunt you too."

True.

CHAPTER FORTY-FIVE

That Didn't Go Well

That did not go the way Garret planned. He paced the floor, his dragon anxious, pulling him to go back to Aquilla. When he saw her in the water, he thought to test her, see if he could provoke her to shift. He didn't expect to fight a snake deity and a dragon who might be stronger than his.

None of this was good. He only wanted to give her the upper hand. Make sure she embraced her full potential and get to the truth of things. He never expected her to be so strong, magnificent, and majestic. He should have known. There was nothing simple about Aquilla, and he had the feeling this was just the beginning of something more, far more.

CHAPTER FORTY-SIX

What Kind Of Lady Do You Like?

Several uneventful days passed. Aquilla woke, ate, trained with Garreth, ate, and slept, but today was special. Today she would see her armor for the first time, and her new sword. She'd asked Garreth to make sure she had the best sword and told him he could go cheap on the armor, but not on the sword. He nodded and waved her off, but she knew he'd heard her.

Aquilla walked into the hall prepared to be amazed but saw nothing. No armor or sword, just Garreth practicing his katas without a shirt. Aquilla thought Garreth wasn't the armor she expected, but he wasn't a cheap second. She stared at him, dumbfounded by the ripples of his muscles that ran up his stomach to his chest. When he brought his sword up, the muscles on his back rippled. Every movement was precise. He gave nothing away. His form was perfect. She stood against the wall and watched him. Aquilla wished she could say she was observing his form, but she couldn't. She had to admit she liked what she saw. Aquilla liked how strong Garreth was and his natural beauty. He laughed easily when they were together. His smile was heart-stopping and awe-inspiring.

She liked how he walked her to the red house every day and told her to be careful on her way back to the inn. He sounded sincere, like he really worried for her safety. Reality came tumbling down, as it always did. Aquilla was a woman dressed in men's clothing, behaving, fighting, and talking like a man. Someone like Garreth could have a woman layered in makeup, heavy perfume, and exposed breasts, which seemed the definition of beauty. Aquilla was none of that. Most of all, the only reason they continued speaking after the caves was because he needed something from her. All of this boiled down to that fact. She was his and her sponsor's tool.

Aquilla pushed herself off the wall and brushed aside thoughts of him that involved anything apart from fighting.

"Hey," she called, and Garreth stopped to face her. He smiled. Aquilla didn't return it. She'd just realized her worth to Garreth, and it stung, even though she knew it shouldn't have.

"Hey, yourself, Aquillo. Your armor is in the back room. I didn't want to distract you during practice, so I put it out of sight."

"That's fine. What are we practicing today?" she asked before she turned her back to him and walked to the wall of swords and staffs. Her anger was unreasonable and ill-timed. She knew it, but still, she couldn't stop herself.

Garreth followed her. She stiffened when he put his hands on her shoulders and kneaded them softly. It should have been awkward since they were both supposed to be two men, but she liked it. She liked him. She'd never been a liar before, and she wasn't going to start now, even if the only person she would have lied to was herself. She liked Garreth, and she wanted him to like her back.

Impossible, he thinks you are a boy. Aquilla, snap out of it.

"What's wrong, Aquillo? You seem tense."

Aquilla sighed. It was a lost cause. There wasn't any reason for a man like Garreth to look twice at a woman who made a convincing boy. She had to focus and push aside things not meant for women like her. She wasn't made to flirt with men. The way her body was made, the things she was interested in, the way she reveled in the fight, weren't ladylike, but it was her.

"I'm fine. I'm just getting eager for the tourney to begin. Tell me again what to expect."

Aquilla moved from under Garreth's hands. He dropped them to his side and stood for a second longer. His mouth was drawn tight in a line of displeasure.

"We talked about the three different competitions, archery, sword fighting and hand to hand combat, but the tricky part is where and what you will have to do during the competitions. For example, archery could be standing and shooting or running through the forest chased by wild boars and shooting at targets. We don't know until the Emperor announces it, but whatever it is, I'm sure you will win easily! So, when you win your last competition, look up to the box seats and say—"

Aquilla cut him off. "Yes, yes, I challenge you and all that. I got that part. Do you know who's arrived for the tourney? Anyone better than me?"

Garreth laughed. "I don't think there's anyone better than you in all the lands. You have a talent for fighting. You can see weakness and kill points as if you see through the core of a person. I don't know how you do it, but I don't think you will have any problems."

Deciding on a long sword, Aquilla walked around Garreth and picked it off the wall. "I didn't become so great by standing around. Let's practice."

HALF AN HOUR LATER, sweat dripped down the sides of Aquilla's face, and she and Garreth were locked in battle. She didn't calculate his next move. She hadn't expected it. Garreth swung back and kicked her in the stomach, hard. Her sword fell from her hand, shocked at the dishonorable hit. On her knees, she gasped for air, "That was not honorable, Garreth. This is a clash of swords, not a showmanship of fisticuffs."

Garreth threw his sword to the ground. "You can't truly believe these men are going to fight fair? I wouldn't put it past them to fight with hands, feet...claws, or have some other trick up their sleeves. Once I saw a man who could tap the side of his handle with two fingers, and a small needle filled with poison would come out. During a fight, the other person wouldn't feel the prick, and within less than ten minutes, his opponent was dead."

Aquilla sat on the ground. She'd caught her breath, but she knew she'd bruise tomorrow. "How dishonorable."

"Not everyone has honor Aquillo. Get up," he said. "Let's practice dishonorable combat."

Aquilla stood and dropped into her fighting stance. She ignored the pain and focused on her opponent.

Garreth's first kick was aimed for her head. She blocked the kick with her arm. She grabbed his leg. She pulled him toward her, trying to make him fall. He fell, and she fell with him, putting her weight into the fall. Aquilla thought when she landed, his leg would twist, and the fight would be over, but he moved, turning, and kicking out his free leg, landing a solid kick to her chest with the heel of his foot. She let go and tried to roll away. He dragged her back, and they wrestled on the ground until he pinned her down and brought his face to hers.

They were so close Aquilla could feel his breaths against her face. Their noses nearly touched. She could see sweat beading his forehead. The weight of his body against hers felt foreign, but she didn't mind it. She couldn't seem to focus on anything except Garreth's lips that curved into a saucy grin. She pulled her eyes away from his lips only to focus on his strong nose and chiseled jawline. Finally, she met his eyes and found him starring down at her. What should she do?

"Do you like other boys?" she asked, then closed her eyes, ready to smack herself in the forehead. Why oh why did she ask that question? Truly, what was wrong with her? And just like that, whatever passed between them was gone, and Garreth was on his back next to her, staring up at the ceiling as she was.

"No, can't say that I do, but a few friends of mine have those types of preferences. Personally, I'm quite fond of women, but I didn't know exactly what type of woman I liked until recently. Do you have a lady you like, Aquillo?"

Aquilla rolled her eyes. This was not what she wanted to talk about. "No. I'm too focused on other things to find someone I'd like."

"Hmm," he said. "Then what type of women do you like? Ones that giggle and fan themselves and complain about everything? I could see you liking that type of lady."

Aquilla thought about it. If she were a boy, would she want a woman full of powder and strong scents? "No, I don't know what type of woman I'd like, but I think she'd have to be strong. I wouldn't want to worry about her."

"So, we are the same there. The woman I like is powerful, independent, responsible, fair, and she makes me laugh without trying, but even though she's strong and could take care of herself, I worry about her. I don't want anything to happen to her. Sometimes, I wish I could throw away all my plans and run off with her far away from the empire and the Emperor. If I could be irresponsible for one minute, it would be to run away with her."

Aquilla felt sad. She didn't know why but knowing that Garreth had a woman he liked made an already impossible situation completely unreachable. She sighed. At least his lady sounded like a sensible woman. He didn't seem like someone who could handle a giggling lady for long. She stood, heartbroken when she shouldn't be.

"She sounds wonderful. I hope things work out for you," Aquilla said and added a half-hearted smile for good measure.

Garreth stood with her. "I don't know. She's close to me but far away at the same time. I need to get her to trust me and believe in me. I want her to understand me and my choices. Why I had to make them and how much I wish I could take most of them back, but I can't tell her any of that, until she opens up to me. What do you think I could do to get her to trust me?"

Aquilla shrugged. How would she know? "I don't know much about relationships, but once Fox, my real fox, bit me, and I was scared of him after that. I didn't want to play with him anymore because I didn't trust him not to hurt me, but still, he came every day and sat next to me. He was far enough that I wasn't afraid but close enough I could see him. He'd just sit there and if I moved he'd follow me, but he'd stay far enough that I wasn't afraid. When I stopped, he did too. Having him there every day all day showed me his loyalty and his sincerity. I began to believe in him a little more every day. Then one day, I went up to him and started playing with him like nothing ever happened. We never parted again until much later." Aquilla hurriedly finished.

"You played with a fox as a child?"

Aquilla nodded and smiled. She missed Fox, but her new human Fox was just as good, if she could pet him, she'd be content.

"Hmm, so you think I should give her time but no matter what don't leave her side and be sincere with my feelings?" Garreth asked.

"It worked for Fox and me. I'd imagine it would work for you. Every creature wants someone."

Garreth nodded. Aquilla didn't want to feel down anymore, and she didn't want to help Garreth get his woman to like him back. Maybe he should just take his shirt off and swing a sword around, and she'd come easy. Aquilla shook her head and asked, "Do you want to go again?"

CHAPTER FORTY-SEVEN

Coincidence

Aquilla stepped outside of the inn after a hearty meal. The sun shone high in the sky like her spirits. Today was the tournament and a good day for fighting. Fox and Berserker sulked behind her.

"By the gods, both of you are ridiculous. You look fine. Nobody will notice you," Aquilla said.

"Berserker doesn't look like a squire, he looks like what he is a man grown," Fox said.

Aquilla looked back. They tried to find clothes that would help with their disguises, but Berserker was such a big man it was hard to disguise him as anything other than himself, much less her squire.

"There's no help for it. We are doing what we must. It's you two who refused to let me go alone, she gave Berserker another look and shrugged. "With any luck, he won't be seen."

"Have you seen him? You can't miss him!" Fox exclaimed then ducked one of Berserker's meaty fists.

Aquilla ignored them and kept walking toward their horses. Berserker was close on her heels.

"Are you afraid?" Berserker asked.

"No, not at all. I'm excited. If the Emperor gathered the best of the best, my skills should be tested, and I can prove I'm the strongest."

"You truly aren't afraid?" he asked again.

"No. I want to get there and put on my armor and test my limits with worthy opponents."

"You realize you're likely the only woman who will fight today, right?"

"Berserker, you're like an old maid nagging me all the time about being a woman this and that. Leave it. I am who I am. Either you accept it, or you don't."

"I do," he said hurriedly. "But, I just fear for you."

"If I'm not afraid, then why should you be?"

"I thought maybe you didn't have enough sense to be afraid."

Aquilla laughed. "Fear will cripple you and make you weak. I learned that the day my father died. I shouldn't have been taken by those men. I'm better than that, but I was fighting more than my enemy that day. I was fighting myself, my grief, my fears, and anger. I won't make that mistake again. I will fight with my heart. Fear not. This night, we will celebrate a day of victories."

"What will you do when it is all over?" Berserker asked.

"Go home," she said. "What about you? What will you do?"

"Visit my sister and mom. After that, I don't know. I haven't given much thought to it. I didn't want to bring this up until after the fight, but I heard this rumor. It keeps popping up here and there. I think you should at least know about it."

Aquilla nodded. "Tell me."

"Fox and I were just minding our business, sitting at the table in the inn enjoying a meal, and these two old drunkards came to the table and asked if we were with Her."

Aquilla glanced at Berserker. He walked next to her, eyes on the ground. "What's that mean?" she asked.

"That's what I said. I told them we weren't traveling with a woman. It was just three men. They nodded and said, 'right, right,' and I thought it was done. Then they said, 'if you were traveling with Aquilla, the lost warrior princess we'd say we were in your service and hopeful change would happen soon,' then they walked away. I asked Fox what those two old men were on about, and he shrugged and said he didn't know anything about it. I left it thinking it was done, but more odd things kept happening."

"Like what?" Aquilla asked. Something tugged her memory, a conversation she'd had, but she couldn't grab it.

"Fox and I went out and traveled the city a bit while you were out at one of your trainings. Every place we stopped, men and women gave us things and called us the blessed warriors. I thought maybe they'd heard of me before from the fights at the cave, so I didn't think anything of it, but Fox, he was not happy about the whispers. He walked right up to a booth and demanded the man to tell him what he knew. The man went on. He said there was a rumor that a lost warrior princess named—"

"Aquilla!" she yelled, interrupting Berserker. She remembered the old shopkeeper's story. "I already heard this story about a princess named Aquilla, grandchild of King Asthmoth who everyone thinks is here to save them from the Emperor. It's too bad I'm going to beat her to it, but I already promised to help her if she ever had a need. Isn't it a coincidence that this princess and I have the same name?"

Behind her, Fox let out a moan. She hadn't known he was listening.

"Coincidence?" Berserker asked.

"Yes, who would have thought me a woman who dresses as a male and wields sword and shield would have the same name as a princess?" Aquilla asked.

"A *warrior* princess," Fox said with heavy emphasis on warrior.

"Do you think she would spar with me?" Aquilla laughed. "Of course not, once I kill the Emperor, she'd become queen. There's no way a queen would spar with me, or even spar at all. No doubt once she has a proper army behind her, she could lay down her sword."

"Would you?" Fox asked.

"Would I what?" Aquilla answered and pointed to the horse shop across the road. At the sight of her horse, her excitement grew; this was really happening. This wasn't the great battle she'd dreamed of, but it was close.

"Would you put your sword down if you became queen?" Fox asked.

"I wouldn't. I would lead my army into the greatest battles of all times," she smiled and turned to Berserker. His face was different. Resigned. She turned to Fox; her smile was so full her cheeks ached. He smiled back.

"Of course you would. I wouldn't expect a different answer," Fox said.

They waited for two carriages to pass before taking the risk of crossing the road to the horse stable.

CHAPTER FORTY-EIGHT

Don't Wink

Garret straightened his cravat. His hands shook. He dropped his arms and balled his hands into fists. He should have told her. He could have told her who he was several times, but he didn't, because he didn't want to ruin the innocent relationship between them. He didn't want her to stop smiling at him. He wanted to delay seeing her big, innocent, hazel eyes look up at him in betrayal, and he didn't want her to think he used her.

But you did, didn't you?

He had a duty to his kingdom before his duty to his heart. He couldn't allow himself to lose sight of the goal because his feelings were entangled with Aquilla. What would she do when she saw him sitting next to his father? What would she think of him? He dared not think too hard on it, or he'd stay in his room like a coward, afraid to offend the woman he liked. And wasn't that the bigger part? He'd finally found someone he liked sincerely. He wanted her for himself, not because of expectations, not because of duty, but because she made him happy. She brightened his days. Every morning over the last fourteen days, he looked forward to seeing her and teasing her.

But all of that was an excuse. He should have told her. He should have been honest with her from the start. But it was too late now. Today was the day, he would expose himself to her piercing hazel eyes and take everything owed to him. He'd shoulder her pain and looks of betrayal.

It was his burden to bear, to do what was right for his kingdom. People were dying because of his father. He couldn't forget that. He couldn't excuse it.

"Come in, Wulf," Garret said before he'd knocked on the door. Garret knew he was there. He knew he'd come.

"Are you ready?"

"No, not at all. She's going to hate me."

"That's likely a true statement."

"I don't want her to hate me."

"You did what you had to do. We found a weapon, and we are wielding it. Yes, her feelings may be hurt, but you saw her dragon. You know she can fight, and she's the only one who can defeat your father. She's strong, stronger than you, and by using her this one time you saved hundreds of thousands of humans. Consider the entire situation."

Garret turned from the mirror toward Wulf, giving up on his cravat. "I know all of this in my mind, but my heart doesn't understand. I just wish there were another way. A way that didn't involve Aquilla."

"There isn't, and we have to do what must be done. I haven't met one king who didn't live without making decisions that went against his personal interests more than once. Being a king is not something I ever envied, but I always understood. I knew early on you would make a great king and a great man, because you did what was right even if it wronged you."

Garret inhaled. "That hasn't changed, and it hasn't gotten any easier. Are my men here and in position?"

Wulf nodded. "Yes."

Garret put a hand on Wulf's shoulder. "Nothing can happen to Aquilla. She must make it out of this alive."

Wulf snorted. "I wouldn't worry overmuch about a dragon with a deity and the son of two snake deities, plus a Berserker behind her. I'm sure they won't let anything happen to her."

Garret smiled. "Especially not that Fox. She's amazing, isn't she?" Garret asked Wulf.

"Indeed. Power gravitates to her and from her. She will make a formidable queen."

Garret moaned. "And then there's that. We'll have to sort that when this is all over."

Wulf laughed. "Good luck with that. Let's go, or we will be late and upset your father and Esmeralda."

"STAND STILL WOMAN," Fox yelled as he chased her around the tent with shoulder guards.

"No, I don't want to wear it!" Aquilla yelled.

"It will stop someone from chopping off your arm!"

"If he could get that close, then I deserve it. No more armor."

Fox dropped the shoulder guards and glared at her. She gave him her sweetest smile in return. The idea of having her own armor was exciting until she tried it on and almost fell over. It was too heavy, and she couldn't be bothered with it all. She conceded to Fox to wear some pieces but not all.

"I have on the chain mail and leg guards, I'm not wearing a helmet. I will wear the breastplate. Where is it?" she asked.

Fox walked to the table and pulled the protective cover off the breastplate. Aquilla's eyes seized on the crest that decorated the front of it. It was an image of a golden dragon roaring, its long tail wrapped around the motto *For valor. We lift our fire with courage.*

"When did this get here? The dragon wasn't on the armor at the hall," Aquilla said as she ran her hand reverently over the breastplate. She looked at Fox, who shrugged. His eyes were bright with amusement. She looked at Berserker, and he shrugged. "Maybe it's a trap," he suggested. Fox hit him.

"Come, it's almost time for the first competition to begin. Let's put on your breastplate," Fox said.

Aquilla did as Fox demanded and turned around. It fit perfectly over her chain mail and wrapped protectively around her.

"We have to go out and get you situated in the arena. Will you be okay from here?" Fox asked.

"Yes, I'm fine. I will grab my sword and follow behind you." Aquilla turned toward the table and pulled the sword out of the elaborately jeweled scabbard. She gripped the sword, feeling the heavy and familiar weight of it. It was beautiful. It wasn't like her father's, and it wasn't quite what she'd dreamed about as a child, but it was beautiful nonetheless. Garreth truly picked out the best he could find.

"I have a gift for you," Mort said in her mind.

"Really?"

"Really."

She felt Mort loosen his grip around her forearm and slide up her hand to the sword, then something magical happened. The hilt of the sword transformed. The guard that was once slightly tilted and curved upward was now straight, and at one end of the guard was a dragon and at the other a snake. The polished silver that matched her armor was less polished. It was rustic with what appeared to be scales a darker color of steel, which ran down the grip to the pommel that stayed the same in its circular shape but changed color to match the steel of the scales that ran down the grip. Then Aquilla looked closer at the pommel. It wasn't the same. The shape was still circular, but the appearance looked more like the tail of a dragon wrapped around than just a steel circle. Mort finished with a hazel jewel in the center of the guard. This was the sword of her dreams. This was the best sword ever made; she knew it. She felt it. Power vibrated through her. She flicked her wrist to test the sword. *Perfect*. She let out a squeak when the jewel in the guard winked at her.

"Don't wink. Don't wink. It is distressing to see your sword wink at you."

"I blinked. I didn't wink. I can't wink," Mort complained.

"Then keep your eye closed."

"I can't see if I do that."

"Then keep your eye open."

"Be reasonable, Aquilla, just don't pay it attention. You're the only one who can see it. To everyone else, I look like a regular jewel."

"Sorry, it just caught me off guard, I'm good now. How do I use you without hurting you?"

"This my final form. The King Killer. You can't hurt me. This form reinforces your sword. I can feed you magic if you need it. I can only change when you are holding the sword. All other times, it will be an illusion."

Aquilla laughed. "King Killer? Did you just make that up?"

"No, promise, my father told me that was my name. His is the King Maker, and my mother is the Undoing. I didn't know my sword name would fit the occasion when I came along with you. I suppose it's fate."

"Right then, Killer, let's do your namesake proud," she said before she walked out of her tent to the arena.

CHAPTER FORTY-NINE

Clever Words

Aquilla heard the cheers of the crowd as she walked into the arena. This was the archery round. Thankfully, no running from wild animals was required. This round, the Emperor wanted them to shoot an apple off a prisoner's head in three different ways. Aquilla didn't like it. Even though they were prisoners, they were still people, which meant some would die in this field if anyone missed.

It wasn't until the crowd quieted that she noticed something was amiss. She looked around. She didn't see anything out of the ordinary. She didn't have anything out of the ordinary. Her bow had the same crest as her breastplate. Maybe they were quieting down because the royal family was joining. She watched the box for her enemy. Someone yelled.

"For valor, we lift our fire with courage."

More joined until it was a chanted all around the Colosseum. Aquilla bit the inside of her cheek, cursing Garreth to the pit of hell and back. She didn't need this type of attention. Who's motto was this?

The man next to her leaned over. "You think because you're allied with the lost warrior princess, you stand a chance? You are nothing but a boy playing games made for men." He spat on her shoe, and she held her control. If this motto were for Aquilla, the lost princess, then she would wear it proudly. After all, she came to do the same things as her.

She wanted to free the people, which Aquilla wanted too, just mixed in with a splash of justifiable vengeance.

"All rise Emperor Athel, Crown Prince Garret, Princess Esmeralda, and King Daemon are entering the colosseum."

Everyone stood. Aquilla watched the door to the box open. First, several guards entered the box, then—then Garreth? No, how could this be? Her hand clenched around her bow.

Liar. He was a liar. He wanted her to kill his father, so he could, what, become emperor? No way. She would see to it that he returned this land to princess Aquilla. This land would never fall into Garret's or his father's hands again. Aquilla noticed the woman. She must be the woman he spoke of during practice. She was beautiful. Aquilla clenched her jaw and closed her eyes against the betrayal. She had to push this away, or it would interfere with her competitions. She repeated the words written on her breastplate.

For valor, we lift our fire with courage, and she did.

When she opened her eyes, the Emperor was staring directly at her; she stared back and lifted her lips in a grin. No fear, there wasn't a reason to be afraid. The Emperor stood and looked out over the crowd.

"Today, we gather to find the greatest swordsman that currently roams my lands enjoy yourselves, and participants, fight bravely. Be bold and victorious."

The Emperor raised his hand. They raised their bows and notched their arrows. They had three arrows for three targets. The first was stationary shooting. Second, running and shooting, and the third diving and shooting all at an apple over a man's head. Once the Emperor's hand lowered, Aquilla let her arrow fly, then she notched another one, jumped off the stand and ran toward her target, shooting as she ran. The crowd cheered her bravery, but she wasn't done yet. She notched another arrow and dived right. She was going to land right next to the targets and let her last arrow pierce every apple on top of the men's heads ending that round for everyone. Aquilla walked off the field, throwing her bow on the ground in anger for Fox to pick up as her squire. If her heart hadn't been ripped open, she would have smiled at the sight of Fox hustling to pick up her bow and retrieve her arrows.

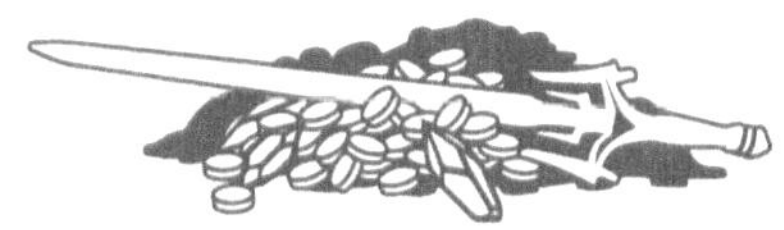

AQUILLA PACED THE FLOOR after telling Fox and Berserker who Garret really was. Berserker tried to reason with her. He tried to tell her that maybe he had a good motive, that he'd done everything right until now. Why would he do that if he meant to hurt her? Fox told her the exact opposite. At least she could trust Fox to be on her side, and with what seemed like joy, Fox cursed Garret, his father, and his lineage at least twice.

"Aquilla, be reasonable. Fox shut up. You aren't helping. She's in the middle of the tourney. She can't be this upset. She will lose focus."

"No, channel it to beat everyone. Anger is only valid if there's an outlet," Fox said.

Aquilla took a deep breath. "How long do we have before the next competition?"

"I would say around two hours," Berserker said, counting off the number of men who still had to go through the first competition and using her rank to determine when she would be called upon next.

"Leave, please, I need to rest." She was bone-weary. Fox and Berserker left. She felt a twinge of guilt. She didn't know where they could go. It wasn't as if they knew people here either, but she needed to let her mind go blank.

"Aquilla." She heard Garret's voice; she smelled his familiar scent. *Traitor*.

Aquilla stayed perfectly still as Garret walked into her tent.

"I know you are awake, and I know you are upset with me. I have a lot to explain, but I don't have a lot of time to do so. I don't like what my father is doing to my people. I wasn't lying about that, but I don't have any other choice to put a stop to him other than you. If I were the one to strike my father down, it would further split the people, and we wouldn't be able to move forward. An outside force had to come in and stop him, so I could claim my birthright and make changes. I didn't know that I would fall in love with you. I didn't know this would hurt so bad, but I must do it. People are dying. So many people, Aquilla, believe in me, please."

Aquilla absorbed his words. Her first thought was that he knew she was a woman all along. Her second thought was he loved her. Her third thought was she didn't believe it.

"I don't trust the words that came out of your mouth, how could I? This could be another way you are trying to manipulate me to continue using me, but you already won, Garret. I'm here playing my role without missing a step. By the time this tourney ends, you will be king. Not emperor. Not here. This land will return to the princess who will rule this land, and if you try to stop her, you will have to go through me first, and frankly, you'd lose."

"You haven't figured it out? Or are you in denial?" Garret asked angrily.

"What are you talking about?" A storm brewed inside her and she knew where to let it out.

"You Aquilla Asthmoth are the lost warrior princess. Don't you see?"

Aquilla laughed. Her life was one disaster after another. First, she thought she was human and denied being a dragon. Now she was for sure a dragon and not human. She couldn't be the lost princess because King Asthmoth was human.

"Trust me, Garret, I'm not the lost princess. There's absolutely no way."

"Why? Because you are a dragon?" he asked.

Aquilla's eyes popped open, and she sat up. Garret paced the floor, running a hand down his face and through his hair. He looked at her. His eyes held guilt, regret, and misery, but then again, he'd been such a great actor up until now. This could be more of the same. Nothing made sense anymore.

"How do you know that?" she asked.

"Because King Asthmoth was a dragon, so was his wife, and so was your mother—and so am I."

If her world had been tilted before, it was upside down now.

"You are a dragon? You knew about me and didn't tell me?"

"No, when we first met, I thought you were human too."

"So, you were going to let a human fight a dragon?"

"I knew you would win."

"How could you know that for sure, Garret? And you knew about my family and didn't think to tell me? Get out. Get out of my tent, get out of my life. I never want to see you again. If I do by the gods, I will take your head myself."

Tears ran down her face. How could all of this happen? Alone, she was completely and utterly alone. Her mother, father, grandparents all gone. All killed by Athel. No more. No more waiting for someone else's plan to play out, no more being manipulated by people. No more letting her people go hungry and her family remain un-avenged.

Now was her time. Right now, right here, she'd take control of her life, and if she really were the lost princess, it was time she claimed her throne.

"Mort."

"Yes," he said. She could feel his pity through their metaphysical link.

"Pity me later, fight with me now." Aquilla grabbed her sword and walked out to the arena. Praying her dragon was with her. At the thought of Lolanthe Aquilla felt a warm embrace wrapped around her soul. She hoped she wouldn't have to become a dragon, but if she did. They would handle it together.

CHAPTER FIFTY

Phoenix

Armed with the King Killer, Aquilla marched to the arena. The crowd calmed in confusion. She walked onto the field and turned toward the men who stood behind her. Their arrows were notched and ready.

"Stand down and move," she demanded.

Her blood roared in her ears. Her heart beat wildly with the thrill of the fight to come. Once the men left, she turned and looked up to the box. The Emperor was on his feet.

She didn't hesitate. "You are a murderer and a coward. You killed my entire family, and you are hurting my people. I will not stand for this another moment."

"Who are you to speak to me, boy?"

Aquilla took a deep breath. Mort must have felt her trepidation. "It's true, Aquilla. You really are the princess. Don't be afraid," he said.

Aquilla took a deep breath and turned to face the crowd. "I am Aquilla Asthmoth, Queen of the Westlands, and I challenge you!"

The crowd roared in approval. The Emperor's face contorted with rage. He nodded his head, and guards flooded the arena.

"Yet you are still a coward, Athel, and you send your guards to capture me because you are afraid of a fair fight. This is the man you all bow down to. This coward!"

"Aquilla, get down!" Fox yelled. She turned. He ran toward her, jumped in the air, and turned into a fox with seven tails almost as big as her dragon. He roared his disapproval at the guards. They stopped their advance. Aquilla was temporarily shocked. Fox was a fox and hadn't told her, then again, she was a dragon, and she hadn't told him, so there was that. Aquilla pulled out the King Killer and pointed it toward Athel.

"Face me and call off your guards, then I will call off my deity."

"You are nothing but a half breed. A human who can't do anything to one as strong as I. You want to face me? You a bastard child of an ill-suited coupling, a monster. Fine, you asked for it."

Fox tensed, ready to fight for her because they both saw he was changing, shifting into something other, his dragon.

"Fox, move far back, right now," She said, reaching up to pet his side. Beneath her hand she felt his tense muscles. He was ready to explode any moment, but he moved back.

"Thank you, friend." She put the King Killer away and searched inside herself. "Lolanthe, I need you." And to Mort she said, "protect the people."

Aquilla gave way to Lolanthe to take control. She felt the shift quick and brutal. Within a blink, she was a dragon roaring fire into the sky. Athel was a green dragon who looked sick. An unnatural darkness clung to him. The two dragons circled each other, snarling, and swinging their lethal tails. Athel struck out first. Lolanthe dodged and brought her tail around, hitting him square in his face. He stumbled then righted himself. They circled each other again. Then Lolanthe struck, going for Athel's neck. She latched on. Blood poured down her mouth. Athel used his claws to pierce her underbelly, but Lolanthe didn't let go, she sunk her teeth in deeper and began swinging her head left and right trying to break his neck, but then Athel flapped his wings pushing dust into Lolanthe's eyes.

"Hold on, Lolanthe," Aquilla said.

She tried, but he got away from her and lifted to fly away. Lolanthe went after him. Her mouth wrapped around his foot, and she threw him back to the ground. He landed on his back. Before he could stand again, Lolanthe landed hard on top of him sinking her right claw deep into his underbelly.

"Where is he?" Lolanthe demanded.

Aquilla was confused, who was he?

"Where is Valin? I can see his taint on you. Tell me."

"I won't tell you anything, but that he's coming for you, he's stronger than you, and this time he will end you for good. You and your mate."

Lolanthe lifted her left foot and brought it down on his chest. Her claws pushed past flesh and bone to prick his heart. With her foot still firmly placed in Athel's chest she breathed a pure blue flame that wrapped around his body, slowly disintegrating bone, and flesh. Lolanthe waited until Athel didn't move again before she pulled her foot out of his chest. His heart was attached to her long claw. As the fire moved up Athel's body, she dropped it in the flame. He would never hurt her people again, and her father could rest in peace.

"We did it!" Aquilla exclaimed. A surge of victory, making them both heady with joy.

"We did little one, or should I say, Queen? Let me help you with something."

Aquilla trusted Lolanthe, she agreed to whatever she wanted to do.

Lolanthe rose into the air. The Colosseum was filled with people, some standing, some sitting, some clapping, some crying, and some angry.

"I'm here to protect you all. Do not be afraid. Dragons of both dark and light still roam the Earth. Some mean you harm, but I am the Queen of this land, and as Queen, I will protect all of my people from harm. None under my banner will need to feel afraid of any dragon that enters my land. My strength is unmatched, and I will wield it to keep you safe. Slowly, together as one whole, we will rebuild what is broken. I have seen your need. I have walked this land, and I am ready to lead. Those who do not want my protection may leave. Leave my land, leave my army, leave my guard, but those who are ready to walk into a new world built from the ashes of the old, follow me."

Lolanthe landed. "The floor is yours now, Little Queen." Lolanthe shifted them to human. Aquilla heard the cheers filled with hope for the future and did what came naturally. With two deities and a dragon, she was sure she could rise from the ashes of her past. She pulled out the King Killer and raised it high in the air and yelled her first victory cry.

To Be Continued in Book 2: Phoenix Flame

Coming Soon visit www.authorsamanthalee.com for more information

Don't miss out!

Visit the website below and you can sign up to receive emails whenever Samantha Lee publishes a new book. There's no charge and no obligation.

https://books2read.com/r/B-A-XNHF-HBCIB

BOOKS 2 READ

Connecting independent readers to independent writers.